"*I forgot to mention the conditions.*"

Eli's collar tightened.

"You can have the *Bethany*, and I'll foot all the bills to convert her, but you have to agree to marry Radcliffe Zahn's daughter before winter." The cane back of Grandfather's chair creaked a bit as he leaned into it and propped his elbows on the arms. He steepled his fingers under his chin and smiled complacently.

Eli met his stare, his mind racing. "And if I refuse?"

"No ship and no funding."

He squeezed his eyes shut and clamped his lips tight. How like his grandfather to connive and manipulate to get his way. Stubborn old goat.

"Why? Why can't you be happy with the way things turned out for Jonathan and Noah and leave me alone?"

"I gave Zahn my word months ago that a wedding would take place. And when a Kennebrae gives his word, he keeps it."

"But you're not keeping it. You're expecting *me* to keep it."

ERICA VETSCH is married to Peter and keeps the company books for the family lumber business. A homeschool mom to Heather and James, Erica loves history, romance, and storytelling. Her ideal vacation is taking her family to out-of-the-way history museums and chatting with curators about local history. She has a bachelor's degree from Calvary Bible College in secondary education: social studies. You can find her on the Web at www.onthewritepath.blogspot.com.

Books by Erica Vetsch

HEARTSONG PRESENTS
HP875—The Bartered Bride
HP887—The Marriage Masquerade
HP900—Clara and the Cowboy

The Engineered Engagement

Erica Vetsch

Barb,
Many
Blessings!

Erica Vetsch

For Georgiana Daniels.
Thank you.

A note from the Author:
I love to hear from my readers! You may correspond with me by writing:

Erica Vetsch
Author Relations
PO Box 721
Uhrichsville, OH 44683

ISBN 978-1-60260-882-5

THE ENGINEERED ENGAGEMENT

All scripture quotations are taken from the King James Version of the Bible.

All of the characters and events in this book are fictitious. Any resemblance to actual persons, living or dead, or to actual events is purely coincidental.

Our mission is to publish and distribute inspirational products offering exceptional value and biblical encouragement to the masses.

PRINTED IN THE U.S.A.

one

"Josephine Zahn. Josie." Her sister's urgent whisper pierced the quiet of the front hall. "Why aren't you dressed? We're going to be late."

Josie glanced up the stairs at Clarice leaning over the banister and made a shushing motion with her hand. She strained to hear the conversation going on in the parlor.

"Radcliffe, you don't seem to grasp the situation. Josephine is brilliant, I tell you, and she should be allowed to continue her schooling. The world needs mathematicians like your daughter." Good old Grandma Bess. Josie twisted her fingers and bit her lip.

"I've said all I'm going to say on this subject. Girls have no need of higher education. I'll thank you not to fill her head with such nonsense—no doubt gleaned from those wretched magazines you insist on bringing into this house. Josephine won't need higher education to run a household, and that's what she's destined for—to marry well and see to the needs of her house and husband. I knew I never should've let you talk me into hiring that engineer to tutor her. I'm tired of tripping over her blueprints and scratch paper, and I'm tired of hearing of trips to the harbor to study the ships. I scotched that behavior quickly. No daughter of mine is going to be hanging around the shipyards, and no daughter of mine is going to go to college."

Josie's heart dropped from her throat to her toes. If Grandma Bess couldn't change Papa's mind, it wasn't going to get changed.

"Jo—*sie*." Clarice spoke louder this time, drawing out the second syllable in admonition.

Josie glanced at the clock and turned away from the parlor doors. Grabbing up her skirts, she bolted up the stairs in a most unladylike manner. "I'll be quick."

Clarice sighed. "We'll be late again. Papa's going to be mad."

"Papa's already mad," Josie muttered. She ducked into her room. Dropping onto the padded stool in front of her dressing table, she unpinned her black hair and picked up her hairbrush. Shrieks from down the hall made her roll her eyes at her reflection. Giselle and Antoinette, ever ready to jump into sister-squabbling chaos.

"They're mine! Give them back!"

"You stole them from me!"

Scuffles and thumps from the nursery.

Josie laid the brush aside and swept her hair back over her shoulders in preparation for going into battle against the younger forces in the house. Before she could rise, little feet thudded on the runner in the hall.

Her door burst open, and Giselle flew in, Antoinette in full chase.

"Josie, help!" Giselle clutched a pair of white kid boots to her chest, her black hair floating wildly around her pale face. Her dark blue eyes pleaded with her older sister.

Josie stood, and Giselle took refuge behind her.

Antoinette put her hands on her hips, panting, cheeks red. "Jo, she's got my shoes. Make her give them to me."

Josie glanced over her shoulder at the enamel mantel clock while she tried to disengage Giselle's grip from her skirt.

The moment Giselle appeared from behind Josie's back, Antoinette made a wild lunge for the coveted footwear. The sprightly Giselle scampered away, leaping onto the canopied bed. The curtains swayed, and the bedsprings creaked. Antoinette's momentum carried her into Josie's desk. A column of books teetered for a moment then crashed to the floor, followed by a cascade of papers. In a final *coup de grâce*, the ink bottle tipped over onto the blotter. Undaunted, Antoinette started after Giselle, who shrieked again—a particular talent of hers—and scooted farther out of reach.

Josie sprang for the ink bottle, scooping it up before the stopper could free itself entirely but garnering a healthy dose of ink on her hand in the process. She held her dripping hand away from herself over the spattered blotter and dug with her clean hand for her handkerchief.

"Girls, stop it this instant!" Mama's voice cut through the chaos like a thunderclap. Everyone froze, Josie included. Mama rarely ventured into the girls' wing of the upstairs.

Josie swallowed hard and clutched her handkerchief over her stained fingers.

Giselle dropped onto her backside on the mattress. Josie almost smiled at the horrified expressions on her younger sisters' faces. To be caught in an unladylike brawl by Mama certainly topped their "worst deeds" list.

Antoinette rushed into speech. "Mama, she took my—"

Giselle's mouth opened for another wail, but Mama's raised hand stopped her mid-inhale.

Mama turned to Josie. "I don't know why you encourage their hoydenish behavior. Whatever their discrepancy is, fix it and do it quietly. I knew it was a mistake to bring them along to this wedding. The social event of the summer is no place for children. But when your father insists, we obey." She looked at the rumpled bed and the glacier-tongue of papers and books on the floor. "This room is a disaster. Why must you always be surrounded by clutter? I have no intention of assigning a maid just to clean up after you. They have more than enough duties as it is. Take care of your own things."

Protest of her innocence in the matter clogged Josie's throat, but she knew it was pointless to argue. Mama saw things the way Mama wanted to see things, and that was that. Josie sent her sisters each a warning glare to keep their mouths shut.

Mama consulted the silver timepiece pinned to her lapel. "We will leave this house in exactly twenty-two minutes. Anyone not downstairs at that time can explain to her father why she made us late." She swept out of the room.

Josie's shoulders sagged, and her chin lowered to her chest. Just like Mama. If one Zahn girl was at fault, all were at fault.

Giselle's lower lip quivered and two blobby tears tumbled down her cheeks.

Antoinette shrugged and stared at the floor. A suspicious moisture appeared at the corners of her eyes. The tongue-lashing Josie had intended to impart evaporated. Antoinette never cried.

"Antoinette, you go first and make it snappy. I'm not even dressed yet, and I don't want to have to explain to Father what made me late."

"She took my shoes. She can't find hers, so she pinched mine."

"Did not! These're mine."

Knowing if she didn't jump in now they'd be back to shouting and chasing each other again, Josie stepped between them, dabbing at the ink blotches on the edge of her hand. "Stop it, both of you. Giselle, give me those shoes."

Giselle handed over one boot then looked about the bed for the other one.

"Well, where is it?"

"I don't know. I must've dropped it." She shrugged, sending a hank of hair sliding over her shoulder and into her eyes.

"You'd lose the Canal Bridge if it was in your possession for two minutes. Give me your foot." Josie grabbed Giselle's ankle and held the boot sole against the little girl's foot. "Look at that. It's way too big. Toni was telling the truth."

"I told you so." Antoinette stuck her tongue out at Giselle and grabbed the boot. "Where's the other one?"

Giselle slid off the bed and shrugged again.

"Well, you had them both when you came in, so help me find it." Josie tossed her soiled handkerchief onto the dressing table.

They found the shoe well back under the bed, though how it had gotten there, Josie couldn't imagine. She had to lie flat on the floor and stretch out until she could grab the heel and drag it out.

"There, order restored, at least to Toni's footwear. Now, both of you, scoot. Giselle, find your shoes. I have to dress."

Antoinette sat on the edge of the bed to put on her boots. While she tugged at the buttons with the buttonhook, Josie opened her wardrobe and pulled out the pale blue dress her mother had chosen. She glanced over her shoulder to her sister. The fabric matched Antoinette's. Mama insisted all her girls dress alike. Josie stuck her tongue out at the despised dress that made her one of the herd.

Antoinette straightened and stuck her foot out, rolling the ankle as much as the high boots would allow. "Stupid old boots." She watched Josie shrug into the dress. "I wish I had my own room like you. Giselle is always taking my things."

"Having your own room doesn't always keep your things safe from little sisters." Josie glanced at the mess of papers and books on the floor. At Antoinette's guilty expression, she laughed. "I know just how you feel, chicken."

She moved to the dressing table to pin up her hair. Getting her black hair into the relaxed bun dictated by current fashion never came easily to Josie. She turned her head this way and that, poking in pins until she was satisfied it looked as near the newspaper clipping of Charles Gibson's "Gibson Girl"—conveniently stuck into the corner of the mirror for reference—as she could make it. She tilted her chin up and lowered her eyelashes, comparing her reflection to the print ad. Who was she kidding? Her face was too round, her nose tilted too much at the tip, and her mouth. . .her lips would never form that perfect little bow.

She turned on the stool and saw her own features, ten years younger, looking back at her from Antoinette's face. "Maybe you can do what I do, Toni. Find little ways to break out, to be your own person." She glanced at the clock. "Let's go. It's almost time."

Josie scooped up her handbag and gloves and followed Antoinette down the stairs. Giselle bounced down the steps ahead of them, hair tied up in pale blue bows and feet shod in her own kid boots. Clarice waited with Mama and Papa in the foyer.

"Line up." Papa's side-whiskers jutted out as he pursed his lips.

Josie prayed for patience as they went through the familiar ritual. Clarice, Josie, Antoinette, and Giselle lined up shoulder to shoulder for his inspection. Four Zahn girls, black of hair, blue of eye, pale of skin.

"Very nice." Papa walked down the line like a general inspecting his troops. "I'm expecting stellar behavior from you young ladies today. This is a momentous occasion, and I want you all there to celebrate it."

Josie shot Clarice a questioning look. Why was Papa so interested in a society wedding? Clarice shrugged and shook her head.

"Now, the carriages are here. Octavia?" He offered his arm. "Bring—" He stopped, frowning and staring at the two youngest girls for a moment.

"Antoinette and Giselle?" Mama prompted.

"Yes, yes, Antoinette and Giselle. I knew that. Though why you had to give them all those fancy French names I'll never know. As if good old-fashioned American names weren't good enough. Should've called them Ann and Jane, like I suggested." He continued this familiar rant out the door to the waiting carriages.

Josie sighed and followed Clarice out into the hot August sunshine. In this one instance she was in complete agreement with her father. Plain old American names would've served them better. But Mama had insisted on French names, and that was that

"Where's Grandma Bess?" She waited for Clarice to climb into the second carriage.

"I'm right here."

Josie smiled as Grandma descended the steps. Here was one woman no one would confuse for someone else. Grandma Bess, tall, spare, ramrod-straight, wore her customary lavender dress with black bead-and-lace trim and wide, swooping black hat with lavender ribbons trailing. Over her arm she carried an enormous black and lavender carpetbag that went everywhere with her.

Josie took her place in the corner of the carriage and looked out as they drove through the streets of Minnesota Point toward the Canal Bridge. She imagined Antoinette and Giselle in the carriage ahead would be squirming with anticipation. They loved riding the gondola across the water.

The steel structure of the bridge loomed ahead. A familiar tightening started in Josie's middle. The five-minute ride on the suspended car across the open water of the canal always made her palms sweat and her heart beat fast.

But that wasn't the only reason her pulse jumped. Every time she thought of seeing *him* again, she found it difficult to breathe. And she'd surely see him today. He was the brother of the groom, after all.

&

Eli Kennebrae twirled his pencil like a baton, walking it up and down his fingers absently as he stared out the window past Grandfather's head.

"Look at me when I'm talking to you." Grandfather smacked the arm of his invalid chair. "You haven't heard a word I've said."

"Yes, I have. I just don't like it. I thought you'd given up on these schemes."

"When has a Kennebrae ever given up? You don't have to like the idea. You just have to do it."

"I don't think so. You don't have the same hold over me you had over Jonathan. As for Noah, well, you're just lucky he fell in love with the girl, or today's wedding wouldn't be happening either."

"No hold over you?" Abraham Kennebrae stiffened, challenge lighting his dark eyes. "I believe I do."

Eli tucked the pencil behind his ear and tapped his papers neatly into a file folder. He leaned back on the settee and propped his ankle on his knee. "And just what is it you think you have that can force me into doing your bidding?"

"I have the *Bethany*."

Eli's leg came down, and he straightened. "What about the *Bethany*? You just agreed I could have her to modify with the new loading and storage system. She's almost repaired to the point where I can start my modifications."

"That's right, I did. But I forgot to mention the conditions."

Eli's collar tightened.

"You can have the *Bethany*, and I'll foot all the bills to convert her, but you have to agree to marry Radcliffe Zahn's daughter before winter." The cane back of Grandfather's chair creaked a bit as he leaned into it and propped his elbows on the arms. He steepled his fingers under his chin and smiled complacently.

Eli met his stare, his mind racing. "And if I refuse?"

"No ship and no funding."

He squeezed his eyes shut and clamped his lips tight. How like his grandfather to connive and manipulate to get his way. Stubborn old goat.

"Why? Why can't you be happy with the way things turned out for Jonathan and Noah and leave me alone?"

"I gave Zahn my word months ago that a wedding would take place. And when a Kennebrae gives his word, he keeps it."

"But you're not keeping it. You're expecting *me* to keep it."

Again Grandfather's hand pounded the arm of his chair. "That's right, I am. Think of it as a business deal, between you and me. You get what you want, I get what I want. Zahn's shipping more than a million board feet of lumber out of Duluth every year. Kennebrae Shipping should have a slice of that pie. Zahn as good as promised that a marriage between the families would guarantee we didn't get just a slice but the whole pie, crust, filling, and meringue."

Lumber, the perfect cargo for his new ship design. If he didn't get the *Bethany* and the money from Grandfather for the modifications, he'd be forced to abandon ideas of building this summer. The year would be spent raising finance and cajoling investors, a job Eli hated. A whole year would be wasted, assuming he could find anyone to back his ideas anyway. Why couldn't he just build ships?

Jonathan ran the family shipping business with an ease Eli could never hope to duplicate. Eli's twin, Noah, captained Kennebrae vessels on the lake, making a name for himself as a hard water captain who feared nothing. And what did Eli do? What mark had he made on the company? Nothing. *Yet.*

But he could, with this new design. All he had to do was say yes to Grandfather's plans. And those plans hadn't worked out too badly for Jonathan and Noah, had they? "I'll think about it."

Grandfather's mouth curled in a satisfied smile. "I knew you'd come around."

"I haven't promised anything. I said I'd *think* about it." Eli stood and gathered his papers. "The wedding is in half an hour. Guess I'd better change."

"She'll be here, you know."

"Who?"

"The girl." Grandfather let out an exasperated breath. "The whole Zahn family is invited."

Eli frowned. This was all happening way too fast. Still, he didn't have time to discuss it further right now. As the best man, he couldn't be late for the wedding. As to meeting his future bride, well, he'd cross that bridge when he came to it. Jonathan and Noah hadn't done too badly for themselves. Perhaps he would be the same.

two

Josie tried not to stare as she stepped down from the carriage in front of Kennebrae House. The massive mansion built of stone filled her view and seemed to blot out the sunshine. *Imposing* was the only possible word for this place. Though she'd never been inside, she'd heard of its impressive opulence.

Her own father's house, *Belle Maison*, named by her mother, was quite impressive, with three stories, a turret, and a wide, inviting porch that looked out upon Lake Superior. Though in a less fashionable part of town out on Minnesota Point, it still rivaled most of the mansions in Duluth. Except this one.

The family ascended the steps in a group, Josie and Grandma Bess bringing up the rear of the line. She wasn't sure what held her back. This day had loomed large in her mind for weeks. Now that it had arrived, she wanted only to duck back into the carriage and speed home.

Pull yourself together. Don't be a silly goose. He probably won't even speak to you.

They stepped into a foyer so grand, Josie sucked in a surprised gasp. *Foyer* was hardly the word for it. To her right and left, a wide area with carved oak paneling stretched through the middle of the house. Before her, across the carpeted expanse, an immense staircase rose to a landing that broke off to the right and left to curve upward to the next floor. On the landing, rainbows of light filtered through stained glass windows featuring swans and lotus flowers in whites and pinks and yellows.

Garlands of greenery and flowers draped the banisters, and

ribbons hung from the wall sconces. The chandeliers—she counted five—lit and further softened the austerity of the room. Women in large hats and impossibly wide-sleeved dresses and men in frock coats and starched white shirts headed to the left.

"Good afternoon, sir." A man Josie assumed was the butler noted the embossed invitation Papa held out for his inspection. "The wedding will take place in the gallery, sir. At the end of the Grand Hall."

Grand Hall. That was certainly the right name for it. Josie fell into line with her sisters and headed toward the far end. Organ music began. Josie searched every face as they entered the room, looking for him while trying not to appear so.

An elbow nudged her ribs. Antoinette pointed up. Light streamed through a gabled glass roof overhead. Oil paintings, some as large as a double quilt, hung in ornate gilded frames on both side walls.

Giselle slipped her hand into Josie's and whispered, "Look at the flowers."

White blossoms—lilies, roses, chrysanthemums, and others Josie couldn't name—nearly obscured the fireplace at the far end of the room. Even from this distance, Josie could smell their fragrance. She squeezed Giselle's hand and bent to say, "Beautiful, aren't they?"

Giselle, a garden lover from birth, nodded, not taking her eyes from the bouquets. Josie had to guide her down the center aisle to the row of white chairs Papa had chosen.

Grandma Bess went in first, followed by Clarice, then Josie, and on down the line until Giselle. Mother sat between Giselle and Papa. Just as she did in church. Just as she always did everywhere.

Antoinette kept craning her neck to look behind them at the organist and the pipes extending up more than two floors above. Clarice, to Josie's left, twisted her handkerchief and chewed her bottom lip.

"Is something wrong?" Josie kept her voice low.

Clarice looked at her lap and gave a short, quick shake of her head.

Josie shrugged. Clarice had always been an intensely private person, keeping her thoughts to herself, holding herself apart from her sisters. Where Antoinette said any and everything that came into her head, where Giselle showed every emotion on her face, Clarice remained aloof and self-contained, always a mystery. Josie went back to watching people.

He came in before she was ready. Following the groom up the far aisle, his presence sent a jolt from the top of her head to the soles of her feet. Her mouth went dry. He was even more handsome than she remembered. Older. After all, it was three—almost four—years since she'd seen him last.

Dark brown hair, smooth and shining, blue eyes that glistened when he laughed, and white teeth that flashed often. That's how she remembered him, smiling, laughing, enjoying himself. He'd teased her a bit, a girl of just fifteen, gauche and uncertain at her first Shipbuilder's Ball. He hadn't danced with her, conferring that honor on Clarice instead, but Josie hadn't really minded. Just watching him had been enough.

Eli Kennebrae. He looked in her direction, his face sober. Her pulse quickened and the butterflies in her stomach turned to seagulls.

The groom, Noah Kennebrae, on the other hand, smiled so wide, Josie wondered if his cheeks ached. Thick brown whiskers covered the lower half of his face. He shifted his weight from foot to foot and clasped and unclasped his hands in front of him, watching the doors at the back of the room.

Pachelbel's Canon swelled out from the organ. Josie lost sight of Eli behind the ostrich feather-adorned hat of the woman in front of her.

Through her misty veil, the bride's smile beamed even brighter than her beautiful golden hair.

Josie didn't pay much attention to the ceremony. She kept her gaze on Eli, noting his broad shoulders, strong profile, and erect stance. Did he still smell of shaving soap? What would it be like to be a bride, walking up the aisle to exchange vows with Eli Kennebrae? She blushed for having such intimate thoughts about a man she barely knew. And yet, the fantasy lingered in her mind.

When the preacher said, "You may now kiss the bride," Noah took his new wife, Anastasia Kennebrae, into his arms and kissed her long enough and with such tenderness that every woman in the room from Grandma Bess to Giselle sighed in satisfaction. Josie caught Mama wiping a tear with her lace handkerchief.

Josie followed her family outside onto the spreading back lawn for the reception. The breeze from the lake cooled her cheeks, though the sun was fierce. Tablecloths fluttered, and more massive bouquets of flowers in urns along the walk enveloped Josie in their perfume.

Expecting to be seated at a table with her younger siblings, Papa surprised Josie by directing her and Clarice to a table of adults.

Her heart jumped into her throat and stayed there.

Eli Kennebrae rose, and his easy smile flowed over her like a warm blanket. "Mr. Zahn." He shook Papa's hand.

"My daughters—" Papa turned to them and hesitated, his brows coming together slightly. "Clarice and Josephine." He smiled broadly, as if relieved to have come up with the answer without a prompt.

Josie winced at the sound of her whole name.

Eli held their chairs for them and made introductions. "My grandfather, Abraham Kennebrae, and family friend, Geoffrey Fordham."

Josie nodded to the elder Mr. Kennebrae. His white hair reflected the sunshine and his black eyes glittered. She had the impression, invalid chair or not, of great strength and mental sharpness. He seemed to miss nothing going on around him. The other man smiled politely at her but made no real impression. Her attention shot back to Eli across the table.

Mama and Grandma Bess took their places, balancing out the numbers. Josie turned to see where her other sisters had gotten to. Giselle and Antoinette sat at a long table near the bottom of the garden, being attended to by a white-coated waiter.

"A lovely wedding, Mr. Kennebrae." Mama smoothed her dress at the waist and tilted her head so her wide-brimmed hat would shade her face. "They're an ideal couple, aren't they? I predict they'll be very happy together."

"I agree. They had some rough sailing, but that's all behind them now." Abraham Kennebrae turned to Grandma Bess. "You're looking well, Elizabeth. It's been some time since I saw you."

"I keep myself busy. Always a lot for a grandmother to do with a houseful of granddaughters."

He grinned. "I have a feeling they won't be underfoot too long. Girls as pretty as these will have suitors hanging about the front gate sooner than you think." He elbowed Eli, who rolled his eyes and looked out over the lake. "Yes, indeed, fine-looking girls you have there, Radcliffe. You should be proud. Shouldn't be surprised if an engagement was announced soon."

"Stop it, Grandfather. This isn't the time or the place." Eli's blue eyes flashed.

Undercurrents sucked around the table like the tide. Josie didn't know where to look or what to do with her hands. Meeting Eli again wasn't supposed to be this awkward.

Eli excused himself from the table as soon as he decently could and mingled with the guests. How could he be thinking of selling his freedom, even for a chance of fulfilling his dreams? Not that he should complain too much. Radcliffe Zahn did have some fine-looking daughters. But it was the principle of the thing that galled him. He couldn't go through with it. He'd tell Grandfather tomorrow. No ship was worth tying himself to a virtual stranger for the rest of his life, no matter how pretty she was.

"Eli Kennebrae?" A short, barrel-chested man with silvery whiskers bristling outward from his cheeks stopped Eli on his way toward the punch table. "Gervase Fox. Glad to know you."

Eli shook the man's hand, surprised at the strength generated by such a small fellow. "Glad you could come."

"Now, don't run away. I've been meaning to talk to you." Fox held Eli's elbow when Eli would've moved on. "I hear you've been in Virginia learning the shipbuilding trade."

"That's right." Eli's interest was caught, as it was whenever shipbuilding came up for discussion.

"Why Virginia? Not enough shipbuilders on the lakes for you to learn from?"

Eli frowned at the challenge in Fox's question but brushed it off. "I wanted to learn the mechanics of oceangoing vessels to see which ones would best apply to lake ships. I'd already studied in the Kennebrae shipyards here."

"And did you learn anything?"

The way Fox leaned in, eyes trained on Eli's face, caused Eli to step back a pace. "A few things, here and there. What did you say you did again?"

"Didn't say. Figured you'd know. I'm Gervase Fox, Keystone Steel and Shipping. Surely your brothers have mentioned me. We're friends, Jonathan, Noah, and I."

"Excuse me, sir." McKay touched Eli's arm, and Eli turned to the Kennebrae butler. "Mr. Kennebrae would like to see you."

"Thank you, McKay. Nice to have met you, Fox." Eli walked away from the little man with the distinct feeling that he was being watched.

Grandfather met him on the back veranda. "Where have you been? It's time for the photographs."

Eli allowed himself to be positioned here and there in the family photos, glad for his brother about the marriage but bored with the proceedings.

Jonathan wore a concerned look and watched his wife, Melissa, like she was a stick of dynamite. Just over a month away from her confinement, Melissa bore his anxiety with good humor.

"How're you holding up?" Eli sat beside her while the photographer set up shots of the bride and groom.

"Fine. It was a lovely wedding. They look so happy, don't they?"

Eli had to agree. The grin hadn't left Noah's face for a month. And his bride couldn't seem to take her eyes off him. A stirring of something—was it jealousy?—flickered in Eli's middle. If he got married, he'd want his bride to look at him like Annie looked at Noah. His resolve to tell Grandfather to call off ideas of an arranged marriage strengthened.

Laughter drew his attention. Geoffrey stood with the two oldest Zahn girls near the table with the wedding cake. Wouldn't it be nice to be Geoffrey, no one trying to force him into marriage, free to just chat with pretty girls on a nice afternoon?

Eli excused himself from Melissa and sauntered over to his friend.

"Almost done?" Geoffrey lifted his chin in the direction of the photographer.

"Yes, though I'm nearly blind with all those flashes." Eli accepted a glass of punch from a passing tray. He looked at the younger Zahn girl over the rim as he drank. Something about her face caught his attention as it had when he first saw her. He liked the way her nose tilted up a bit at the end and the way her lashes fringed her blue eyes. Why did she seem so familiar to him? Had they met somewhere before?

"I think I'll stroll down toward the water," Geoffrey spoke to no one in particular. "Would you care to join me, Miss Zahn?" Geoff held out his arm to the older Zahn girl—Clarice, wasn't it?

She nodded and accepted his offered arm, leaving Eli standing with her sister.

He set his cup on the table behind him. "Josephine, right?"

She winced. "Please, call me Josie. Josephine always makes me feel like a pet poodle on a satin pillow."

He grinned. "Josie it is, then. I hate to be so forward, but I feel as if we've met somewhere before."

The way her eyes lit up told him he'd been right. "Yes, we have, though I'm surprised you remember. It was some years ago." She flicked a glance up at him through her lashes then looked out over the lake once more. Captivating.

"Some years ago? Let's see. Was it at the yacht races? No?" He cast back in his mind. "Founder's Day Picnic?"

She shook her head and hooked her little finger through a strand of hair that had blown across her cheek. He studied the curve of her jaw and the slender column of her neck before dragging his mind back to the question at hand. "I'm sorry. You'll have to jog my memory."

"The Shipbuilder's Ball of '03."

He snapped his fingers. "That's where it was. We danced together, didn't we?"

Her expression went from happy to sad in an instant, like snuffing out a candle. "No, that was my sister. You danced with Clarice that night."

❧

Josie stood on the front lawn and watched the bridal couple

drive away. Women waved handkerchiefs and men clapped. She prayed they could go home soon. No matter how she looked at it, it always came up the same. She would always and forever be just one of the Zahn girls, interchangeable, identical in everyone's eyes. The moment Eli had confused her with her sister, it was like someone had set a cold sadiron on her heart and left it there, pushing all the life out of her. Would he, or anyone else, ever see her as an individual?

That Eli, of all people, had done it only made it hurt more. And yet, could she blame him? It had been a long time ago, and she and Clarice did look so much alike. Perhaps she should solace herself with the fact that he remembered that night at all.

Her gaze found him, leaning against the gatepost, talking to his friend, Mr. Fordham. His hands gestured as he spoke, and Mr. Fordham laughed. They must be good friends.

The tinkling of a bell caught her attention. The Kennebrae butler stood on the front steps beckoning the guests near. Beside him, Abraham Kennebrae sat stately and proud. On the far side of the invalid chair stood her father. Puzzlement knit Josie's brow as she moved to stand with the others to hear what they had to say.

Her mother edged close and clasped her arm, drawing her through the crowd to stand at the front of the semi-circle of guests. Josie found herself in her familiar spot in line between Clarice and Antoinette, a place both comforting and exasperating at the same time.

"Ladies and gentlemen." Their host cleared his throat. "We didn't want to take any of the attention away from the bridal couple, so we waited until their departure to make this announcement." He motioned to Papa, who stepped forward, smiling.

"It is with great pleasure that I announce the engagement of my daughter—" He paused and looked frantically down at the row of girls in pale blue.

Josie's breath stuck in her throat, and all thought ceased. Her heart beat against her ribs like a captured bird, and her mouth went dry. Engagement?

Her father continued, "Clarice to Eli Kennebrae."

All the air whooshed out of Josie's lungs.

Clarice gave a strangled little cry of surprise.

Papa beamed. "Come up here, Clarice, Eli." He beckoned.

Mama gave Clarice a shove to get her started.

Clarice moved as if in a dream.

Josie knew exactly how she felt. This whole day had been a nightmare.

three

A band of steel settled around Josie's forehead and tightened a little with each new comment from her parents.

"A fall wedding, don't you think?"

"Consolidating the shipping makes sense."

"I hear charmeuse is the new thing for wedding gowns. But I think you should get married in silk."

"Abraham and I have been planning this for over a year."

"Do you think we should have the wedding at Belle Maison or at Kennebrae House? Today's wedding was so lovely, but I want my girl married at her own home."

And so it went on through their arrival home and continued all through the light supper. A supper neither Josie nor Clarice was able to choke down.

Josie looked at Clarice again. Her sister sat as if in a stupor, eyes blank with shock. Josie knew just how she felt. A lightning bolt from a clear blue sky couldn't have hit with more surprise.

Clarice was engaged. To Eli Kennebrae.

Josie looked to Grandma Bess to see how she was taking the situation. Grandma sat in her customary chair, paying no attention to the ebb and flow of conversation going on around her, totally engrossed in one of her magazines. How could she read her serial stories at a time like this?

Josie wanted to stand and scream at her parents for being so cruel. How could they just spring this on everyone? And why did it have to be Eli?

Josie's train of thought stopped when she realized everyone was looking at her. She didn't remember getting to her feet.

"You wanted to say something, Josephine?" Mama raised her eyebrows expectantly.

Heat coursed through Josie's face and neck and spun in her ears. "It's been such a big day. I think I'm developing a headache. May I be excused, please?"

"Yes, of course, and Clarice, you may go, too. We'll talk more in the morning."

Josie dragged herself up to her room. The mess of papers and books beside the desk remained. She had no energy or enthusiasm to clean it up. It would have to wait until morning. And with her tutoring cut off and no hope of college, why bother to keep the books out anyway?

She was turning back the rumpled comforter and getting ready to climb into bed when someone tapped on the door.

Clarice entered when Josie called.

Surprised, Josie slid into bed and pulled the covers up over her lap. Clarice wasn't one for midnight confidences, though Josie supposed if ever she needed someone to talk to, it would be now.

Clarice sat on the end of the bed and leaned against the footboard, pulling her knees up and tucking her toes under the hem of her dressing gown. "I can't believe any of this is happening." She grabbed the cuffs of her sleeves and put the heels of her hands up to cover her eyes.

"I know. Didn't they give you any warning at all?"

"None. I nearly fainted. How could they do this to me?" Clarice dragged her hands down her face. Her black hair hung in twin braids on her shoulders.

Josie hadn't bothered to braid her hair for the night, too mixed up in her emotions for such a mundane task. Evidently not even a cataclysmic shock could keep Clarice from her evening routine.

"What are you going to do?" The question had burned in Josie's mind for hours.

"What *can* I do?" Clarice's brow wrinkled. "I don't see that I have a choice in the matter."

Josie shrugged. It was an impossible situation. A formal engagement had been announced in front of nearly a hundred witnesses. Mama and Papa were thrilled with the match. And what Mama and Papa wanted, Mama and Papa got. Clarice was right. She had no choice.

"This is terrible." A tear slipped down Clarice's cheek.

Josie watched it glisten in the light of the bedside lamp, and her own eyes filled. She blinked hard, hating to cry even worse than Antoinette did.

Clarice's shoulders shook. "I don't love him."

"Of course you don't. You barely know him." Josie no sooner said the words than she had to chide herself. *You barely know him either, and you've been in love with him for more than three years.*

"You don't understand. I love someone else." The words seemed wrung from Clarice. She put her forehead down on her knees.

Josie blinked. The self-contained and ultra-private Clarice in love? "Who?" Josie leaned forward.

Clarice shook her head, either unable to tell or unwilling. Her muffled sobs continued.

Josie sat back against the pillows and stared at the organza curtains of the canopy bed. What a mess. Clarice engaged to the man Josie wanted. . .and in love with someone else altogether.

⋇

As family dinners went, Eli had to judge theirs less than a success. His anger carried him through the first two courses, and Grandfather thrashed him verbally until he was goaded into responding in kind.

Melissa finally laid down her fork and leveled them both with a glare that reminded him of Grandmother back when

Eli was a young boy. "Enough, both of you. Grandfather, I thought you'd finally learned your lesson about these engagements, but I see you need another dose of humility. Be careful the Lord doesn't teach it to you. And, Eli, stop saying such terrible things you'll regret. Nothing will be settled tonight. Either finish your supper in peace, or leave the table so Jonathan and I can."

The anger simmering in Jonathan's eyes at them for upsetting Melissa in her delicate condition drove Eli from the table like a naughty child. Good thing after all that wedding food he wasn't very hungry anyway.

Eli entered his workroom and paused to let the familiarity of his sanctuary sink in. He leaned against the door and crossed his arms, his eyes taking in the familiar drafting table, bookcases, and shabby, overstuffed chair by the small fireplace. The eaves sloped down on two sides, but the wide window permitted sunlight to fall across the desk for most of the day. Though darkness had fallen hours ago, he still sought his attic workroom as a safe port in the storm.

McKay must've anticipated his need. The lamp on the mantel flickered and a pot of coffee sat on the table beside the chair. That man had an uncanny ability to serve that amazed and humbled Eli.

Eli dropped into the chair, allowing its familiar comfort to soothe the tense muscles in his neck, and poured himself a cup. He drew the warm fragrance deep into his lungs and tried to relax. He hadn't been able to think clearly since Grandfather had dropped the cat amongst the pigeons at the reception. Always a deliberate thinker, Eli needed quiet and time to process what had transpired and what he was prepared to do about it. He should've anticipated this move from Grandfather—making the engagement public so no one could back out. The old man had pulled it on both Eli's older brothers to varying degrees.

The door creaked open, and Geoffrey's head came around the edge. "Eli?"

"Come in." Eli made to stand.

Geoff motioned him back. "McKay told me you'd be up here." He stepped into the room and looked around. "Nice bolt-hole you've got. Wish I had someplace like it."

Eli put down his coffee cup and gathered up the books and papers littering the footstool. It was the only other place to sit, since Eli always stood to work at the drafting table.

McKay tapped on the door and entered with a small tray holding another coffee cup.

Again Eli was amazed at the man's ability to do the right thing at the right time. "Thank you, McKay."

Geoff waited until the butler had closed the door before he looked at Eli. "Wanted to see how you were holding up after such a big day." He blew across his coffee cup and took a sip.

Eli shrugged. "He ambushed me."

"He ambushed all of us—again."

"Humph. I told Grandfather I'd think about it. *Think* about it. I didn't know today was the day. And I have the distinct feeling that the girl didn't know it either. She turned to a pillar of salt when they trotted out their announcement." Eli shifted in his chair, remembering her ghost-like pallor and trembling hands. "Either it was a tremendous shock to her or distinctly unflattering toward me as a prospective husband." He tried to raise a smile from Geoff, but the lawyer's expression didn't change.

"What do you think of her?"

"What's to think?" Eli spread his hands wide in a helpless gesture. "I don't know her. I've barely spoken to her. I shared more words with her younger sister today than with Clarice herself."

"Will you go through with it?" Geoff leaned forward, elbows on knees, his stare boring into Eli.

"I hardly know where I am at the moment. The engagement has been announced. Now I know just how my brothers felt when Grandfather pulled this stunt on them. And I'm just as trussed up. If I back out now, not only will the girl's reputation be called into question, but I'll lose—" He hesitated, not wanting Geoffrey to know he'd been contemplating exchanging matrimony for a chance to fulfill his dreams. What had he been thinking to let Grandfather maneuver him into this corner? One moment of weakness, and the old man had pounced.

"You'll lose what?"

"My self-respect," he substituted lamely. "When a Kennebrae gives his word, he keeps it." The irony of using Grandfather's own words stung him enough to make him laugh bitterly.

Again, Geoffrey didn't share the humor.

"Let's talk about something else."

"What? What else is there?" Geoff's coffee cup hit the table hard enough to slosh some of the liquid out over the rim.

"Let's talk about my ship." Eli shoved aside thoughts of matrimony and machinations in favor of metal and machinery, an infinitely more interesting and safer subject to consider. "I have the preliminary drawings done and the go-ahead to start the work, but I'm having trouble with some of the calculations." He rose and picked up his latest sketches. "I'm no mathematical genius. I can do the basic stuff, but I need some help with calculating the stress on these beams here and just how much I'll need to reinforce the hull here and here to compensate for the removal of this angle support and this one." He pointed to the cross-section of the hull. "And I'll need to recalculate the other measurements, now that I have an actual ship to use."

Geoffrey joined him at the table but hardly seemed to be listening. A muscle flexed in his jaw, and his hand gripped the edge of the drawing.

Eli sorted through the chart rack beside the drawing table. "I've studied her blueprints a little bit, just based on the repairs I knew were underway, but I haven't fit my ideas to her quite yet." He tugged out the drawings of the *Bethany* and unrolled them. "I'd sure like to find someone to go over the calculations for me. I need someone who can keep his mouth shut. My design is going to revolutionize lumber shipping, and I want to keep it quiet until I launch the ship." His mind skipped ahead to that glorious day when the ship would come off the ways and he would make his mark on the shipping industry. And he would become a valuable member of Kennebrae Shipping at last. "Keep your ear open for me. If you come across someone you think could help, let me know." He rolled out another schematic. "What do you think?"

"I think it's monstrous." The words shot out of Geoffrey's mouth like bullets from a gun.

"What?" Eli's head came up.

"What you Kennebraes do to people. You treat folks like pawns, pushing them here and there, making them do things they don't want to do, just to get yourself ahead. I know it's worked out for Jonathan and Noah, but what happened today—" Geoffrey broke off. "I'm sorry." His lips were so stiff, Eli could barely understand him. "I've said too much." He blew out a breath, his shoulders sagging. "I know today wasn't your doing. It was your grandfather, as it usually is. You know, when it happened to Jonathan, I thought it was funny. Even when Noah got led a merry chase by Annie, I thought it a lark. But today, I suddenly had it to the back teeth. People shouldn't be treated this way."

Eli turned around and leaned against the table, crossing his arms on his chest. "I know. I just don't know how to change things."

Geoffrey had never spoken so vehemently about anything not business related. In the boardroom or the courtroom,

Geoff was a tiger, fighting on behalf of his client for all he was worth, but anywhere else, he was as easygoing a man as one could find anywhere. To see him so upset drove home what an impossible situation Eli was in.

Geoff smacked Eli on the back, an apologetic look lingering in his expression. "I'd better go before I jeopardize my job as legal counsel to the Kennebraes."

"Like that could ever happen." The idea made Eli smile. "You're the only one who gets along with all of us at the same time. Grandfather will never let you go. In fact, if you're not careful, he might find a bride for you, too."

four

"Sit up straight, Josephine. You look like a wilting vine." Mama tapped her palm with her closed fan. "Proper young ladies must have impeccable posture at all times." She snapped the fan open and fluttered it below her chin. "Once more, if you please, from the beginning."

Josie sighed and straightened her spine. Listening to an instrument or singer was pleasant but having to play as her sisters performed chafed. She liked music theory well enough but couldn't carry a tune in a valise with the clasp padlocked. Her mother had relegated her to playing the piano while her sisters sang.

She cast a longing glance through the music room window toward the lake then turned her attention back to the lesson. Antoinette's sweet soprano held a note, while Giselle's little girl voice chimed in. Though Josie cocked her ear ever so slightly toward Clarice, she couldn't hear any of the song from that direction. Clarice hadn't said a word this morning about the engagement. Her already pale skin looked even whiter, and her eyes showed the strain of sleeplessness.

"That's fine, ladies. You may go now." Mama levered herself to her feet when the song finally ended. "Clarice and Josephine, I'd like you to stay. We have further lessons to accomplish today."

Josie tucked her lips in and stifled another sigh. These infernal daily etiquette lessons would send her mad before too long. She spun on the piano stool and put her feet side by side under her hem.

Clarice sat on the chaise, not allowing her back to touch

the puffy, beribboned pillows leaning along the wall behind her. Her hands lay in her lap, and her downcast lashes hid her expression. All she would tell Josie about the man she loved was that she had met him at the Lyceum and they had arranged to meet there several times through the opera season. No one in the Zahn household liked opera save for Clarice, but because Mama thought it a status symbol, she'd allowed Clarice to attend through the winter in the company of several girls from her class. Now Clarice's shoulders slumped in defeat.

Josie frowned. If it was her, she'd fight. She'd stand up to Mama and Papa. No way would she allow them to push her into a marriage.

"Just a few things I wanted to go over." Mama lifted a book from the table beside the door. Her movement set the bead fringe around the lampshade swinging. "Clarice, you're an engaged woman now."

Clarice flinched, and Josie tried to ignore the pain that jabbed just under her heart at Mama's words.

Mama continued. "You'll be inundated with callers and opportunities to attend social functions. We shan't give anyone reason to cavil at our social skills. That's why we're going to study each and every chapter of *Mrs. Catherine Morris's Proper Etiquette for All Occasions.*" Mama tapped the book in her lap.

Josie put her elbows on her knees and propped her chin in her hands. "Why do I have to be here? I'm not engaged."

"For the tenth time, sit up straight. I despair of you, child. And keep your chin level with the floor. You will be accompanying your sister on many of her outings, especially those Eli Kennebrae cannot attend, or to ladies' only events like teas and the garden club. It wouldn't do for Clarice to attend alone, nor should she attend with only her mother as company. Besides, this will make an excellent entrance for you into societal circles we've only just begun to crack. We may well find a suitable match for you as a result."

"So I'm to be part of Clarice's entourage so you can trot me out to potential buyers?" Outrage flowed through Josie's limbs. She had no trouble straightening her back or keeping her chin level with the floor.

"Modulate your voice. You know full well Mrs. Morris insists a lady must always keep her tone civil and her words sweet."

Josie bit the inside of her cheek to keep from pointing out that Mama's own voice was less than civil or sweet at the moment.

Grandma Bess entered the room, her footsteps slow, leaning heavily on her cane. Her black bag thumped against her side. "Octavia, I hope you don't mind if I take a chair in here. I was out on the veranda, but the breeze became too strong."

Mama smiled, but tight lines formed at the corners of her mouth. "Of course I don't mind, Mother Zahn." The lines deepened when Grandma took the chair between Mama and Clarice and dug in her bag until she found her latest periodical.

"A new magazine arrived in the post today. I just have to find out what happened to the countess. She was in a dreadful bind when the story left off last month."

Josie craned her neck to see the cover picture. *Ainslee's*, *Atlantic Monthly*, *The Monthly Story Magazine*, *Saturday Evening Post*, Grandma subscribed to them all, and several more. Much to Mama's despair, Grandma insisted on speaking of the "lurid characters," as Mama called them, in the serial stories as if they were real people.

"Clarice, I've had new calling cards printed for you. They should arrive this afternoon. Also, we need to make plans for your trousseau. Evening wear and tea gowns first. Then sporting costumes, day dresses, and undergarments."

Clarice, who adored new clothes, only nodded.

Josie let her mind drift from the conversation to a particularly stubborn geometry problem she'd encountered in one of her books. Perhaps she was approaching it wrong. She often found if she backed off a problem and started from another angle, the solution would come to her. If only real life were as organized and simple as mathematics. If only she had her tutor to talk to. But he'd moved to Detroit when Papa fired him. Poor Mr. Clement.

Mother leaned over and rapped Josie on the knee with her fan. "Josephine, stop wool-gathering. If you don't learn these rules, you'll perform a frightful gaffe in front of the wrong people, and that will be the end of your hopes of a fine match. Why must you always daydream when important matters are being discussed?"

"Important to you maybe," Josie muttered under her breath.

"Josephine!" Mama reared back and glared. "That will be quite enough from you. You are excused. If you wind up an old maid because no one will marry such an uncivilized, disobedient horror, don't blame me."

Heat suffused Josie's cheeks. She knew better than to talk back to Mama, and yet she did it time and again. She caught Grandma's eye.

Grandma gave her a slow, deliberate wink then buried her nose in her magazine again.

Josie rose, nodded to Mama, and escaped to the library.

❧

Late afternoon sun fell across the book in Josie's lap. She sat curled in a wide wingback chair, her geometry book and tablet in her lap, feet tucked under her hem. The library was the one place in the house where she could almost always be alone. The little girls felt at liberty to wander—or run—in and out of her room all day for the slightest reason. But the dark, quiet, scholarly atmosphere of Papa's library held no appeal for them.

She really should formulate her apology to Mama for talking back, but it was so hard to drum up the proper humility. Mama could exasperate Josie so quickly. Sometimes Josie wondered if she had been dropped into the wrong family by mistake. She might look like her siblings, but often she felt a stranger in their midst. Only Grandma Bess really seemed to understand her or see her as an individual. But that was probably only because they were both so often in trouble with Mama.

The library door opened behind her, rubbing on the Aubusson rug Mama was so proud of. Josie froze, hoping whoever it was would go away. Nobody could see her from the door, hidden as she was by the high back of the chair, and, if she stayed quiet, would probably leave.

"No one will see us in here. It's the one place we can be alone." Clarice. Who would she be bringing to the library?

"Are you sure? I'd be hard-pressed to explain my presence if we're discovered."

Josie's mouth dropped open. A man's voice. Her fingers curled around the edge of her book. Curiosity feathered up her arms.

"No one but Josie ever comes in here. I don't know why Papa even put a library in the house, except it's expected for rich men to have one. I've never seen him crack a book."

Josie kept her breathing shallow. It sounded as if they'd moved to stand almost directly behind her chair. Should she interrupt?

"Enough about your papa. Clarice, it's been torturous. What are we going to do?"

"I don't know. There's nothing we can do. It's too late." The flat, fatalistic tone of Clarice's voice caused sadness to weigh down Josie's chest.

"I don't believe that. There has to be something. I'm going to speak to your father."

Where had she heard that voice before? It tantalized her, just at the edge of her memory.

"It won't do any good. Papa doesn't change his mind. And anyway, there's your job to consider. If you speak up, the Kennebraes will fire you."

He worked for the Kennebraes?

"I don't care. Clarice, I can't live without you. I love you."

The rustling of movement and steps on the carpet, and Josie could tell Clarice was being embraced. In an instant she knew she shouldn't be hearing this, that she was eavesdropping in the worst way. But how could she get out of the room without their knowing?

"Please, Geoffrey, don't. It only makes it harder."

Geoffrey, that's who it was, the man who had been with Eli at the wedding reception.

"Harder? I don't see how it can be. I'd like to shake you, Clarice. How can you even dream of going through with this? I know you love me. You must."

Josie leaned over and dropped her book flat on the hearth. It smacked, and the sound ricocheted off the glass-front bookcases surrounding the room.

Clarice squealed.

Geoffrey rounded the chair, his hands fisted.

Josie blinked and stretched like a cat waking up, then shook her head as if surprised to see a man before her. "Hello." She put her hand up to cover a fake yawn. "Do I know you?"

"Josie!" Clarice crossed her arms at her waist, her lower lip darting behind her teeth for a moment as she looked at Geoffrey then back at Josie. "Stop pretending you were asleep and didn't hear a thing. I know you better." She pointed to the book. "You never fall asleep over math."

Josie shrugged and straightened. She'd tried to give them a graceful way of saving face. It wasn't her fault if Clarice didn't take it.

Geoffrey shoved his hands into his pockets, his face like a thundercloud. "So much for a private place to talk. Getting a Zahn girl away from her sisters is impossible."

Josie put her tablet on her math book and stood. "So I gather this is the man you met at the opera?"

Clarice nodded and stepped closer to Geoffrey. "Geoffrey Fordham, this is Josie."

He nodded but didn't take his eyes off Clarice. He looked like a man dying of thirst and she was a tall glass of water. "There has to be something we can do. I went to talk to Eli about it last night, but I had to leave before I punched him in the teeth."

"Why? What did he say?" The words leaped out before Josie could stop them. It really was none of her business. In fact, she should find a way to escape, but mention of Eli kept her rooted to the rug.

"He's so busy with his shipbuilding plans, I wonder if he even knows he's engaged. All he could talk about was his ship and his math problems." Disgust laced Geoffrey's words. "He's engaged to the woman I love, and he acts like he doesn't even care."

"Math problems? What math problems?" Josie's mind leaped up to chase the idea.

"Who cares? Something about his new ship design. He had the gall to ask me to help him find a mathematician, when all I wanted to do was throttle him for treating Clarice so cavalierly." Geoffrey paced to the window and back.

Clarice stopped him from repeating his steps by placing her hand on his arm.

He took it and tucked it into his elbow.

"What did you expect him to do?" Josie asked. "He barely

knows her. It would've made you madder if he'd have pretended he was in love with her. If Eli didn't know the engagement would be announced, then he's as much a victim as Clarice. Perhaps he's coping the only way he knows how."

Geoffrey gave Josie a curious glance, and she realized how hotly she'd come to Eli's defense. Embarrassment heated her cheeks and climbed into her ears.

"I suppose you're right. If he knew about Clarice and me, he'd feel terrible. We've been friends a long time. He'd never steal another man's girl." He patted Clarice's hand and squeezed it close to his body with his elbow. "The question is, how can we fix this?"

Josie tapped her chin. "I doubt it will be Eli you need to pacify. It will be Mama and Papa and old Mr. Kennebrae. They're the ones who cooked up this batch of catastrophe."

Clarice pulled her hand away from Geoffrey's grasp. "Stop it, you two. There's nothing we can do. I can't defy Mama and Papa." Her blue eyes looked agonized, but her expression was resolute. She moistened her lips and crossed her arms at her waist again. "I'm sorry, Geoffrey. You know how I feel about you, but I cannot go against my parents' wishes." She didn't cry, but her voice broke at the end. She turned and fled.

Geoffrey took a step to follow her, but Josie stopped him. "Don't. She's upset. She's like Papa. Once she makes up her mind, it's awfully hard to change it, especially right away. Let her cool down. Maybe there's a way out of this." She plopped down in the chair and put her elbows on her knees, defying Mama's nagging about posture that echoed in her head. Her chin rested in her palms, and she nodded for Geoffrey to sit in the opposite chair. "Tell me more about Eli's math situation."

He perched on the edge of the chair and looked toward the door. "I don't want to talk about math. I want to know what to do to get Clarice to change her mind and back out of this engagement."

"Maybe one is related to another." An idea, or the ghost of an idea, flitted on the edge of Josie's mind.

"How?"

"What you need now is time. Time for Clarice to get her courage up. Time to figure out what you're going to do. If you keep Eli focused on his ship, he'd have less time to spend with Clarice, and you'd have more time to map out a plan of attack. All you need is a mathematician to keep him busy."

"And where am I going to get one of those? They don't grow on all the bushes around here."

"How about me?" She spread her hands wide.

"You?" Geoffrey smiled then quelled it, looking at her in a patronizing way she was so familiar with when a man found out she liked math. "This is a little more complicated than figuring out needed yard goods for a ball gown or converting a recipe for two to feed a dinner party of twelve."

Josie took a deep breath, then bent to her tablet, flipped through a couple of pages, and turned it to face him. "This isn't exactly recipe conversions. Although I can do those, too."

He took the tablet and frowned at the rows of numbers and symbols. "What is this?"

"It's a line graph for flow dynamics. I was calculating the approximate rate of flow of water past a whaleback ship's bow versus a conventional steamer's bow."

"A line graph?"

"A handy tool for solving complex equations."

"And you can do this? Nobody's helping you?" He leafed through the pages.

She shrugged. "I've always been good at math. I guess you could say I think in numbers. You could write to my tutor, Mr. Clement, if you doubt my abilities. He taught me for over two years, though most of it was theoretical study when Papa forbade me to go to the shipyards anymore."

"You could do what Eli's looking for? He wants help

calculating stress loads and hull bracing, and I don't know what all."

Her mind raced with the possibilities. Helping Eli, helping Clarice and Geoffrey, and getting to work on an actual ship—real-world problems. A hint of doubt nudged her. Real-world problems required real-world solutions. And being wrong held consequences. But she wanted to try.

"The dilemma will lie in keeping my identity a secret. You're a perfect example. No man is going to think a woman is capable of the complicated mathematics necessary for structural engineering."

"And how can we keep your identity a secret? He's bound to notice you're a girl." Geoffrey tunneled his fingers through his hair in exasperation.

"Then we'll just have to make sure he doesn't find out."

five

Enough wooden scaffolding shrouded the *Bethany* as to resemble a log jam in spring. Eli mounted the ramp and climbed toward the deck.

Jonathan's footsteps scraped behind him. "Have you been to see her yet?"

"No. Not yet." Eli ignored both his brother's snort and the nasty nudge his conscience gave him. "I've been busy."

"Too busy to go see your fiancée?"

Eli climbed faster, as if he could outrace Jonathan's pestering. The immense cleft amidships came into view. "She sure hit that shoal hard. The surf nearly broke her in two." Eli stopped for a moment to survey the damage. "I don't know how you survived."

Jonathan paused beside him and shuddered, though the August sun beamed down and a soft breeze flowed through the shipyard, cooled by the lake. "God's mercy. A lot of good men didn't survive that storm."

"Must've been hard, being so close to land and still so far from safety."

"The longest night of my life." Jonathan turned away to watch a man scurry up a ladder near the smokestack, his shoulders bowed under an immense coil of rope.

Eli sensed his brother was done talking about it. Both Jonathan and Noah had little to say about the events of that night, and Eli supposed he didn't blame them. Things could've gone much differently during that storm.

Jonathan crossed his arms. "You didn't say when you were going to go see Clarice. Don't you think you should make some time in your busy schedule?"

"I will. Like I said, I've been busy." Eli turned his back and headed up the next ramp.

They reached the deck near the pilothouse, their footsteps echoing on the metal decking.

"She looks about down to scrap iron right now, but just you wait. You won't even know her when I'm done." Eli patted the building plans rolled up under his arm.

"You haven't said just what you're doing to change her." Jonathan stuck his head into the pilothouse, his expression sober. For a long moment he stared at the tiny space, no doubt reliving moments of the previous November when the ship had grounded just outside the safety of the harbor, a victim of the worst storm in Duluth's history.

"Come into the chartroom, and I'll give you a quick peek." Eli shouldered the door open farther and stepped inside the wheelhouse. He ducked his head to enter the small room just behind and spread his papers on the chart table.

Jonathan followed and leaned against railing guarding the steep steps to the hold.

"Which dock job pays the most?" Eli reached for two books to weigh down the edges of the curling blueprints.

"Lumber loaders," Jonathan answered quickly. "Every stick loaded by hand. Hard work. They deserve the pay. One of the reasons we've steered clear of hauling lumber, though I suppose with your marriage that will change."

Eli grimaced and sighed. "Look here. This is a plan for a typical lumber hooker. One hundred sixty feet long, thirty feet wide. In order to make hauling lumber efficient, a shipper usually has a steamer and a tow barge, loaded to the gunwales, with lumber stacked on the deck and in the hold." He loosened the edge of the plan, and it rolled across the table to reveal the sheet underneath. "But look at this. The *Bethany* is four hundred fifty feet long. Her capacity for lumber would be huge."

Jonathan scanned the drawing, already shaking his head. "The labor to load and unload her would erase any profit for filling her with pine. No doubt she'd hold a lot, but it would all be for nothing if you couldn't turn a profit. And she'd be laid up in the harbor for days on every trip. It would take a full crew of lumber loaders several days to fill her up. Add another several days at the other end to unload her, and you've really bottomed out the number of trips she could make in a season."

Eli grinned. "Exactly. But that's if you're loading her by hand. What if I told you I had a design that would allow you to load her by crane, and in less than five hours?"

"I'd say you're barmy." Jonathan straightened away from the chart table and crossed his arms. "But I'd be willing to listen to more."

Eli grabbed a pencil from the mug in the rack on the wall and, with a few strokes, sketched out his design. "Look, if we alter the deck hatches, it would allow enough access that an entire unit of lumber could be lowered at one time. Then, I plan to add a sliding storage system to move the lumber from side to side in the ship. By orchestrating the loading process, you could balance the lumber as you loaded it, lock it into place on the sliders, and *voilà*!"

Jonathan scratched his chin, his dark eyes keen on the sketch. "And you've thought all this out? It's really possible?"

A grimace tugged Eli's mouth, and he used the end of the pencil to scratch his hairline. "In theory. The math is a little fuzzy, but I'm working on that. It just needs a few kinks ironed out. I need to hit on just the right hatch construction that will open wide but close down to be watertight. But think what it would mean, not just to Kennebrae Shipping but to the lumbermen of Minnesota and all over the Great Lakes. Fast, efficient ways to get their lumber to purchasers."

His older brother looked thoughtful. "If it worked, it would revolutionize the industry."

"That's what I aim to do. Put Kennebrae Shipping on the map as the leader in Great Lakes shipping. And this invention and this ship will lead the way."

A knock rang on the open metal door, and Gervase Fox stepped in. "Afternoon, boys." His stare darted into every crevasse of the room, and he rubbed his hands together in relish. "Hope you don't mind my coming here to see you. I was over at my own shipyard and thought I'd stop by to see how repairs were coming on the *Bethany*."

Jonathan stepped forward, all but crowding Gervase in the small space, shielding the chart table from prying eyes.

Eli quickly picked up the books and allowed the drawings to roll up with a dry rustle.

"Gervase, just the man I wanted to see." Jonathan stuck out his hand. "I've been meaning to ask you to dine with me at the club. I want to hear all the news about this new ship you're building at your yard. Word has it she'll dwarf anything else on the lake. You'll have to be careful you don't build her so big you can't get her through the Soo Lock." He herded Gervase to the door, and before he exited, he shot a warning glance over his shoulder.

Eli nodded. Their footsteps rang on the deck, and as soon as Eli could no longer hear them, he grabbed his plans and headed down the steps to the hold.

A man in filthy overalls lay on his back half in one of the boiler fireboxes, his boots braced on the floor, his torso straining. Metal clanked on metal. The smell of coal dust, oil, and iron filled the air.

"Hey!" Eli had to shout above the noise. He leaned over the rail from the catwalk.

The man jerked then wriggled out of the hole. His expression cleared when he looked up at Eli. "Mr. Kennebrae, sir." Soot streaked his large features and coated his bald head. "Just checking the fireboxes are still sound. I know it ain't a job for a foreman, but I figured I'd feel better if I looked them over myself." He rubbed his hands on his thighs.

"Gates"—Eli rolled his papers tighter—"I want you to see that a guard is installed at the shipyard gates. Nobody in or out who isn't a Kennebrae employee. There are plenty of shippers who'd give a considerable amount if they knew what we were doing here."

"Twenty-four hours?"

"Twenty-four hours a day until this ship slides off the ways."

❧

Josie followed Grandma Bess and Clarice into the next gallery. Sunlight streamed from high windows, bathing the room with natural light that picked out all the bright colors of the paintings on the walls.

"Look at this one. I love the way the mischief shines out of that little boy's eyes." Grandma lifted her lorgnette and peered at a painting of a boy and his dog.

Josie tilted her head to look down the long room and into the next. More paintings.

Clarice passed to the next frame but appeared not to see the arrangement of fruit and flowers portrayed there. She refused to talk to Josie about Geoffrey or her engagement, wandering the house like a ghost. Mama fretted over her lack of appetite, and Grandma Bess pursed her lips and lowered her brows whenever she encountered Clarice in the house. The outing had been Grandma's idea.

"Isn't it amazing? I had no idea there were so many women artists of this caliber." Grandma consulted her catalogue. "And wasn't it clever of the Duluth Women's Suffrage League to bring this exhibition here to raise money for the cause? I hear Melissa Kennebrae headed up the committee and arranged for the gallery space."

At the mention of the Kennebrae name, Clarice started out of her trance.

The now-familiar jab poked Josie's heart. It had happened so often this week, she wondered—if she could see her heart—whether it would look as bruised and battered as it felt.

"Just imagine, all these women striking out to make their mark in what has always been considered a man's field." Grandma's cane tapped on the shiny wooden floor as she made her way to the next painting. "And they've done so with grace and dignity. Two qualities to be admired in any woman."

Clarice nodded, her carriage becoming more erect. "I intend to be a woman of grace and dignity, too. 'Above all else, cultivate a gracious and courteous demeanor at all times.' And I intend to make Mama and Papa proud of me."

Josie grimaced and tugged at her gloves. Another quote from Mrs. Morris's book. Clarice was beginning to sound just like Mama. They practically ate that book for breakfast.

"Another quality I admire, though, is bravery. These women are brave."

"Brave? How scary is it to paint pictures of pears and puppies?" Josie shrugged and edged toward the door. She had no more interest or talent for painting than she had for singing. She wanted to get home to see if there was any word from Geoff about Eli's plans.

"On the contrary, child. These paintings took a particular brand of bravery. Bravery on the part of a woman to be who God made her to be. To use the talents He's given her for His glory and the betterment of mankind." Grandma shot Josie a pointed look. "It took a lot for these women to paint these fine pictures—confidence in their own abilities, a willingness to risk the condemnation of their male counterparts, and vulnerability to exhibit their work for the comments and criticism of the general public."

"You make it sound like a battle." Josie looked at the oil landscape in front her with new interest.

"It is a battle, dear, this struggle to be the women we were created to be. The tide is changing in America, but though the doors are opening for women, we must be careful how we charge through them. To rampage, to hurl ourselves against the male establishment, is to invite their scorn, to be treated as the hysterical females we're acting like." Grandma lowered herself to a bench and stacked her hands on her cane. The long ostrich feather decorating her hat wafted with her movements. "But my granddaughters"—she smiled at them—"are smarter than that. They have grace and dignity, as these women artists do. They will find ways to ensure men see them for the treasures they are, women of intelligence, ability, and sense, with God-given talents to be exercised and appreciated."

Josie mulled over her words as they walked the remaining galleries. If she could paint like these ladies or sing or sew. . .or do anything as well as these ladies, maybe she'd be brave, too.

"And how are your mathematical studies coming along now that you've outgrown Clement's instruction?" Grandma peered through her eyeglasses at a seascape, her back to Josie.

"Fine."

"Have you ever considered what God wants you to do with your skills?"

"What can I do with them? Papa forbids higher education." Josie stared at a herd of fat cows in a meadow. "Without a degree, no one will take me seriously. And women in mathematics are more rare than quiet when Giselle's around."

"Nonsense, child. Have you heard nothing I've said? God didn't make a mistake when He gave you that brain, and He expects you to use it." Grandma huffed in impatience. "Come along. All this walking has made me tired, and we don't want to miss the last tram down the hill."

Josie followed after her, confused and somehow dissatisfied with herself and the afternoon. Would Grandma consider a little clandestine mathematical consulting work to be using her talents wisely?

six

Eli shoved a box of books out of the way with his foot and sagged into the new leather chair, allowing the smell of the upholstery to surround him. Why had he let Jonathan talk him into moving his office into the Kennebrae Building? Sure, it was closer to the shipyard, but was the upheaval worth it? Though he admitted to a small thrust of satisfaction seeing his name in gold letters on a door at Kennebrae Shipping, he hardly felt as if he deserved it—yet.

Eli hated change almost as much as he hated the time it took away from his plans for the *Bethany*. He really should see that everything was organized in here before delving into the designs again, but the drafting table pulled at him, beckoning him to get a new idea on paper before he lost it. Ignoring the books, papers, and boxes on the floor, Eli headed to his charts to jot the idea down. It would only take a minute or two, and he could get back to clearing away this mess and have his office organized by noon.

A knock startled him out of his concentration, and he glanced at the wall clock by the door, surprised that more than three hours had passed.

Geoff opened the door and stepped in, weaving around the clutter. "Looks like the aftermath of Bull Run in here." The lawyer picked up a wooden ship model poking out of a carton. "McKay said you'd be tinkering at the drafting table instead of tidying up. Guess he knows you pretty well. I got the impression he was itching to get in here and put things to rights." He set the model on the mantel and stepped back, clunking into a pile of books.

Eli rubbed the side of his head and yawned, relaxing his jaw after such a long period of intense concentration. He rolled his shoulders and flexed the fingers of his writing hand. "Sometimes I lose track of time. I'll get it shipshape. Anyway, having visited your office, I know firsthand you're not the tidiest lawyer in town."

Geoff grinned and picked up a book, scanned the spine, and replaced it. "Is that any way to treat a man who comes bearing gifts?"

"Gifts? Well, in that case, your office is impeccable. I wouldn't change a thing." Eli shifted a rolled-up rug off a chair and beckoned Geoff to sit. "What gift?"

The chair creaked like a new saddle. "You are in need of a mathematician, I believe?"

Eli's heart thumped. "You've found someone?"

"I found someone." He laced his fingers across his vest and stuck his feet out to the cold hearth. "Professor Zechariah Josephson."

"A math professor? Perfect. When can I meet him, show him the plans?"

Geoff studied the tips of his shoes. "We–ell," he drew the word out, "that might be a problem. You see, Professor Josephson is a recluse, preferring to work alone in his study. He doesn't entertain visitors and rarely leaves his house. He's interested in your project, but all correspondence would have to take place through me to preserve his privacy."

Refusal hovered on Eli's lips. "How can we work together if we can't even go over the plans face-to-face? And where did you find this fellow anyway? Do you trust him? Is he any good at what he does?"

Geoff coughed and cleared his throat, then stared at his fingertips. "He's a friend of a friend, and I've seen some of his work. Complicated stuff—flow dynamics, load equations, stuff like that. Way over my head, but he's confident he can help you. But remaining at arm's length is unconditional. He won't have his privacy invaded. You write out in detail what it is you're trying to accomplish, give me the notes and a copy of your drawings, and I'll deliver them to Professor Josephson. When the calculations are ready, I'll bring them to you."

Impossible. Design a ship with a partner he'd never met? And yet, secrecy was of utmost importance. Who better than a recluse who never left his house? Eli spent a second wondering what Grandfather and Jonathan would say then thrust that line of thought aside. It was his project, his design. He could choose whomever he wanted to work on it. After all, it had cost him a pretty penny to achieve—engagement to a woman he barely knew.

"All right, we'll try it. It will take me a couple days to get some notes together. Is the professor local? Will it take much time to get the plans to him?"

Again Geoff contemplated his shoes. "I can have it to him in under an hour from the time you give them to me."

Eli sat back. "That will make it easier, though I'm surprised I haven't heard of this Professor Josephson. Has he done much work in the area of ship design?" Doubts trickled into his mind.

"Why don't you just try him out? If the project doesn't go like you'd hoped, you can always call things off."

Too much was riding on this to call it off. The respect of his grandfather and his brothers, the chance to do what he'd always dreamed of doing, the chance to earn this spacious office he'd been given just because his name was Kennebrae. No, he wouldn't call it off.

The signal on the desk buzzed.

Eli levered himself out of his chair and flipped the switch to the new intercom system Grandfather had installed the previous winter. "Yes?"

"Mr. Kennebrae, there's a Mr. Fox here to see you."

Eli sighed and put his palm on the back of his neck. "Send him to the boardroom. I'll meet him there."

"Gervase Fox?" Geoff rose.

"Yes. That man is everywhere. He pops up like a gopher every time I turn around. Come with me to see what he wants."

They entered the boardroom through the private entrance from the Kennebrae office suite to find Gervase standing with his hands clasped below a life-sized oil painting of Abraham Kennebrae in his prime—before his stroke. Abraham stood tall and straight in the picture, his black eyes seeming alive and full of fire, his broad shoulders and strong hands indicative of the power of his mind and will. The portrait had long intimidated Eli, and when he found himself in this room, he usually maneuvered to sit where he couldn't see it.

Fox turned and smiled. The sight of so many teeth gave Eli the willies, and he braced himself for the man's aggressive handshake. "Eli, thank you for meeting with me."

Eli noted the use of his first name with irony. They weren't on a first-name basis, but he decided to play along. "Gervase, what brings you down here?" The Duluth offices of Keystone Steel and Shipping were in a less prestigious part of town than the Kennebrae offices.

"You, son. I want to discuss the repair and refit on the *Bethany*. I'm interested in those modifications, and I'm willing to pay top dollar for them. Not only that, but I'm offering you a job as my ship designer. And I'm willing to pay top dollar for you as well." He named a sum that caused Eli's head to reel.

Geoff sucked in a gasp, and when Eli darted a look at his lawyer, Geoff's face took a moment to return to its usual politely interested expression.

"That's a lot of money, Gervase, and I do appreciate the

offer, but I'm afraid I couldn't possibly leave Kennebrae Shipping." Eli leaned against the back of one of the tall chairs flanking the table, trying to appear more relaxed than he felt.

"Don't be a fool. You won't get that much a year from any-place else, and you're low man on the totem pole around here. Jonathan will inherit, and where will you be? Noah's set, marrying money like he did. But you, you're engaged to a woman who is one of a gaggle of females. Whatever her father settles on her at her marriage is likely to be all you get. He's got a fleet of girls to launch, and a lot of dowries to pay. Zahn's rich, but he isn't that rich. I'm offering you a sizeable sum for your ideas and a great deal more for your services." Gervase's eyes glittered much like Abraham's in the portrait over his head. "Tell him, Fordham. Tell him what a fair offer I'm making."

Geoff's brows had come down, and red climbed his cheeks. His hands shook slightly.

Eli's heart warmed to see Geoff so angry on his behalf. "Geoff doesn't have to say anything. I can make up my own mind. You've got a lot of nerve thinking you can buy me like you buy a trainload of wheat or a shipload of ore. I'm not for sale, Mr. *Fox*." He trod hard upon the name, emphasizing his desire to distance himself from the odious little man. "Geoff, would you be so kind as to show Mr. Fox out then come back to my office for those plans. I'd like to get them delivered as soon as possible."

Gervase's face smoothed out, but his eyes hardened. "I hope you don't regret your decision, young man. Keystone Steel and Shipping *will* be the biggest company on the lakes, and Kennebrae Shipping will be trying to keep up. Your grandfather and brothers have stood in my way long enough." He turned on his heel and strode out, slamming the door so hard behind him, the frosted glass pane vibrated in his wake.

Josie followed Grandma Bess into the pew at the Kennebraes' church, feeling acutely the gap where Clarice should be sitting. Clarice sat in the row before them at Mama's insistence. Right beside Eli, her fiancé. Mama insisted they all attend here this morning. Didn't want to miss a single congratulation, no doubt.

Organ music swelled out as people found their seats. Normally, Josie would've taken in all the details of the sanctuary, it being her first time at this church, but she was so miserable sitting so close to Eli and having him out of her reach, she couldn't muster the curiosity.

Josie leaned forward slightly and saw Antoinette elbow Giselle. Mama quelled them both, and Josie sat back. All of them were attired in rose dresses with ivory lace trim. Antoinette and Giselle wore ivory pinafores, but aside from that, all four girls looked identical. Josie thumbed through the songbook and wished she had coppery red hair or dusky olive skin or eyes black as an Ojibwe, something, *anything*, to be different, to stand out from her sisters and be noticed as more than just one of the Zahn girls.

The reverend took his place in the pulpit and motioned for the congregation to stand and join in the first hymn.

Eli stood and angled his body to share a hymnal with Clarice. Clarice held herself rigid, keeping space between them at all times. If it had been Josie, she'd have inched as close as she dared, just to be near him, to feel the warmth of his arm pressed to hers, perhaps to let their fingers touch.

Grandma Bess tugged Josie's sleeve. She started and realized the song had ended and everyone else had resumed their seats. Red hot embarrassment scuttled up her cheeks, and she plopped into the pew.

"Our text for today is found in the Psalms, chapter 139 and verse 16. 'Thine eyes did see my substance, yet being unperfect; and in thy book all my members were written, which in continuance were fashioned, when as yet there was none of them.' David knew that God had planned his existence long before David ever drew his first breath. Jesse, David's father, had many sons—strong, brave, handsome sons. Seven of them passed before Samuel, and yet God didn't choose any of them to be king. He chose David, whom He had equipped specifically for kingship before David was even born."

Josie's attention wandered from contemplating Eli's broad shoulders to center on the reverend. Poor David. Seven brothers. Three sisters were bad enough.

The preacher expounded on how unique David was within his own large family, and how God had given him special abilities.

And he wasn't afraid to use them. Not against bears, lions, or giants of the Philistines. Josie ran her thumbnail along the edge of her open Bible in her lap. *He wasn't afraid to be the man God made him to be.* Visions of the paintings from the exhibition floated in her mind. All those women who used their talents. Grandma's admiration for them. Josie's own desire to study higher mathematics and use her talents and gifts. David didn't let anyone keep him from using his gifts. Resolve began to harden in her.

The service ended before Josie was ready, before she'd pursued to the end all her thoughts on the passage. When the reverend voiced the final prayer, Josie added her own to it.

God, I know You made me just the way I am, and You gave me a love of mathematics. Help me to put aside my feelings for Eli and concentrate on being the woman you made me to be. Help me to use my talents for Your glory, like David did. Amen.

She stood to sing the doxology, more peaceful in spirit than she could remember being in a long time. Though her heart squeezed in a vise of longing tinged with regret, she kept her eyes focused on the pulpit. Eli would have to cease to matter to her. She couldn't be a serious mathematician and be mooning over her sister's fiancé at the same time. She'd just have to put him out of her mind.

"Eli, you will join us for dinner? You and your grandfather?" Mama made the request sound like a command.

Josie's peace cracked like lake ice during the spring thaw. This was going to be harder than she thought.

Clarice shot an imploring glance over Josie's shoulder. Josie turned to see Geoffrey, his hands fisted at his sides. Apprehension twisted her middle. Having all of them in such close proximity reminded her of the subterfuge they'd entered into. Her conscience protested. Here she stood in the house of God, deceiving everyone around her in one form or another.

Dinner would be a nightmare.

seven

As it turned out, Sunday dinner differed little from any other. A messenger had arrived at the church as they were exiting, whispering to Mr. Kennebrae and departing.

"You'll have to excuse us, Mrs. Zahn." Mr. Kennebrae motioned for his carriage to be brought up. "It seems my grandchild has chosen to make his appearance nearly a month early. We must get back to Kennebrae House to await his arrival."

Eli had assisted his grandfather into the coach and departed with hardly a backward glance.

When the family trooped home, Clarice went straight to bed with a headache. Mama fussed and flitted, and mid-afternoon sent Josie up with a cup of tea to check on Clarice.

Josie tapped on the door and entered. Though the pulled shades shrouded the room in darkness, she walked confidently. The furnishings exactly matched those in Josie's own room; in this aspect, too, Mama expected them to be identical. The only marked difference was the desk. Clarice's desktop was bare, not a pencil, not a book, not so much as a box of stationery. Josie couldn't remember the last time she'd seen the entire top of her own desk. "Mama sent up some chamomile. How's your head?" She directed the comments to the lump under the covers.

The bundle shifted, and Clarice's face appeared in the gloom. "The head's fine."

Josie set the tea tray on the dressing table and sank onto the bed. "Useful things, headaches." She laced her fingers around the post at the foot of the bed and leaned back.

58

"Keeps you from having to do all sorts of things."

"Humph. If it would keep me from having to marry Eli Kennebrae, I'd come down with a migraine for the rest of my adult life."

Josie pursed her lips. "I've come to a decision today. You want to hear what it is? It might take your mind off things for a while."

Clarice scooched up to rest against the mounds of lacy pillows. Her knees bent up to form a slope of bedspread. "Nothing will take my mind off things, but go ahead. I can see you're dying to tell me."

"I'm going to be the woman God made me to be." Josie couldn't keep the triumph out of her voice.

"Congratulations." Clarice looped her arms around her shins and rested her chin on her knees. She gave Josie a dubious look.

"No, seriously. I've decided to be like those painters we saw this week. I'm going to go to college and study mathematics."

Clarice rolled her eyes and shook her head. "Don't be silly. You can't go to college. Papa would have a fit, not to mention the absolute earthquake Mama would cause. And where will you get the money? Papa won't pay your tuition. 'Women have no business studying beyond what is necessary for running a household and raising children,'" Clarice intoned, deepening her voice in a fairly good imitation of Papa.

"I don't care. I'll find a way. Didn't you listen this morning? The reverend said we needed to use our talents like David did. God-given ability should be used for God's glory."

Clarice ran her tongue over her upper teeth and thought for a moment. "God also says obey your parents."

Josie flopped backward on the bed, wincing as her hairpins poked the back of her head. "What if your parents are wrong? Sometimes doing the right thing means you have to go against other people's ideas of what is right. David did what was right, even when his brothers didn't like it. He faced down a giant who was defying God. David knew what he had to do, and he did it in spite of opposition." She scowled at the canopy. "Mama and Papa can try to fit me into their mold of a 'proper young lady,' but I don't have to let them succeed."

Clarice wrapped her arms tighter around her legs and stared at the little bump her toes formed under the covers. "I wish I had your courage, Josie."

❧

Matthew Abraham Kennebrae arrived less than an hour after Eli and Grandfather made it home from church. The doctor, packing his bag, smiled and shook his head. "Mighty quick labor for a first child."

Grandfather wheeled his chair close to Melissa's side and peered at the swaddled bundle in her arms. "You're sure he's healthy? And Melissa, too? He's on the early side by a few weeks."

"Sound as a dollar. Though I can't say the same for Jonathan." The doctor looked over the rims of his glasses to where Jonathan lay sprawled in a chair. "His missus did well, and she'll be back on her feet in no time. It's the husbands who can't stand up under the strain."

Melissa motioned for Eli to step close. "Here, you should hold him. Everyone else has had a turn."

Eli backed up a step. "No, no. He's too little. I wouldn't want to break him." His mouth went dry at the very thought.

"He's a Kennebrae. They don't break so easily." Melissa bent a loving look on the squeaking, grunting infant. Her eyes glowed in a way that made Eli's chest feel full and empty at the same time. He found himself stepping forward and accepting his nephew into his arms.

It was like holding air. The baby regarded him solemnly with hazy dark blue eyes. Eli's heart constricted for a moment. What would it be like to hold his own son? To cradle his heir and offspring and feel a tide of love and protectiveness crash over him? A whole little person in his arms. A miracle, right in front of his eyes.

"That's enough." The doctor took the baby and placed him in the crib beside the bed. "Mrs. Kennebrae needs her rest. She can't get it with you men in here."

Grandfather went to his bedroom to rest before dinner, while Eli headed to the parlor. He would spend the afternoon working on the sketches for the hatch mechanisms until dinner was ready. Jonathan followed, too keyed up to settle to anything.

An hour later, Eli wished he'd gone to the office. Jonathan wouldn't leave off talking, and becoming a new father seemed to make him an expert on marriage and family.

"You need to take this seriously. Ignoring the situation won't make it go away." Jonathan tossed the newspaper down on the footstool.

Eli put his pencil down and looked over his shoulder. "Who says I'm not taking it seriously?"

"I do. Every time I broach the subject, you skitter away like a bug on a stove lid. Marriage is serious business. It changes your whole life. Or at least it should. I bet you haven't spent more than five minutes considering the ramifications of marrying Clarice Zahn. How did Grandfather maneuver you into this engagement in the first place? What did he offer you?" As if he couldn't bear to be still another minute, Jonathan sprang up and paced the salon carpet. He clasped his hands together behind his back and lowered his chin.

Eli sighed and turned on his chair until he could rest his arm along the back. "That's between Grandfather and me, and who's to say it won't all work out fine? It sure did for you and for Noah."

Jonathan stopped and put his hands on his waist. "Your

treatment of your fiancée is atrocious. You haven't spent more than an hour in her presence, and most of that time was in church. You have no idea if you'll be compatible. If I'd have treated Melissa in such a callous manner, our marriage would be a nightmare, and I'd have no one to blame but myself."

Eli shifted in his chair. "What do you expect from me? Grandfather arranged this marriage. It isn't as if I have to court the woman. And frankly, I get the distinct impression the lady would prefer me to keep my distance."

The fact chafed. Clarice had barely spoken to him this morning. When he'd offered his arm to see her out of church, she acted as if a timber rattler had slithered past her fingers. "I asked her if everything was all right, and she said, 'Fine.'"

Jonathan snorted. "If there's one thing I've learned from being married to Melissa, it's that when a woman says things are fine, it never means fine. If Melissa says she's fine, I'm usually in trouble. 'Fine' has a million meanings to a woman, and none of them match up to what it says in Webster's."

Eli tilted his head and cocked an eyebrow. "So what do you suggest I do?"

"Spend some time with Clarice. Figure out how she feels about the whole thing. Take her out, get to know her. She seems like a nice girl. And above all else, to save your sanity and the peace of your future marriage, find out what she means when she says, 'Fine.'"

The task of unraveling a woman's thought processes boggled Eli's mind. Why couldn't they be straightforward, like men? Eli knew where he was with a man. Like Gervase Fox. He got directly to the point. And Eli had been just as blunt in reply. No secrets, no hidden meanings, just straight shooting.

"They shouldn't make things so complicated." Eli stood and gathered up the papers he'd been working on. "I'm going to my room to work. I can't concentrate here."

Jonathan shook his head, eyeing Eli gravely. "Trust me, Eli. You're going to have to put some effort into this relationship before you take her as your wife. Your life and hers will be miserable if you don't."

&

Josie strolled down the canal pier, listening to the slap of waves against the pilings, wishing she could pull the pins from her upswept hair. A pleasant breeze teased the tendrils along her temples and nape. The high lace collar of her afternoon gown itched just below her jawline.

Clarice walked beside her, careful to shield her face from the sun with her parasol. All traces of her headache had disappeared the moment Josie suggested this excursion. "What time were you supposed to meet him?"

Gulls sailed and swooped overhead, squabbling and calling. Josie checked the watch pinned to her lapel. "He said six o'clock in his note. We're a few minutes early."

"Why did he want to meet you in the harbor? It isn't a very nice place. Why not in one of the parks?" Clarice sidestepped two gulls fighting over a piece of garbage. "It's so dirty down here." She tugged her lace gloves on more firmly.

Josie stopped to lean on the concrete wall. She loved the harbor, the sights, the smells, the sounds. Even on a late Sunday afternoon, Duluth Harbor hummed with energy. The lake surged with a life of its own, ever different, ever the same. She peered into the brownish blue water of the canal. A mama mallard bobbed on the waves, her clutch of ducklings like a small flotilla behind her, paddling furiously to keep up. Their tiny peeps made Josie smile. A brave mama indeed to take her babies out on the massive water, and yet they looked content enough.

"Geoffrey said he would explain when he got here." Josie wondered at the wisdom of bringing Clarice. She couldn't escape the fact that she was somehow abetting her sister in being unfaithful to Eli. But that was silly. Neither had sought the engagement they found themselves in. And what harm could come from Geoff and Clarice meeting in a public place like the harbor, especially with Josie in tow?

"There he is." Clarice's cheeks flushed, and her eyes took on a glow Josie had never seen before.

Geoff strode toward them, the breeze ruffling his hair, his long strides eating up the distance between them. He held a rolled-up bunch of papers clamped under his arm, and his hands were thrust deep into his pockets. When he arrived, he had eyes only for Clarice. His Adam's apple lurched, and Josie had the uncomfortable feeling that she was witnessing something deeply private.

Clarice's mouth trembled.

A shaft of sympathy arced through Josie. She knew what it was to be in love with someone out of her reach. Knowing she was intruding, Josie turned her back and contemplated the ducks again. *God, how did we wind up in this mess? They are so in love. How can it be wrong for them to be together? But what of Eli? What would he say if he knew?* She shoved aside her guilt and cleared her throat, turning around to face Geoff and Clarice.

Geoff seemed to realize for the first time that Josie was there. Faint ruddiness climbed his neck, and he touched the brim of his hat. "Hey there, Professor."

"Are those for me?" Josie motioned to the papers.

He took them out and handed them to her. "Schematics, supply lists, and here's an envelope with notes from Eli." A thick brown envelope appeared from inside his coat. "I picked them up on the way down here. Big uproar at Kennebrae House. Abraham's fit to burst his buttons. He has a great-grandson."

Was Eli as happy as his grandfather? As close as he seemed to his brothers, he must be happy for Jonathan and Melissa.

Josie had to remind herself that she wasn't supposed to feel this glad. It wasn't as if she were part of the Kennebrae family. How deeply ingrained thoughts of Eli had become. This infatuation had to end. Eli was engaged to Clarice, and Josie had best get used to the idea. The wind fluttered the edges of the rolled-up papers, reminding her why she was here.

"Did Eli say when he expected a reply?" Josie turned and laid the plans on the wall, anxious to get her first peek at the design. She anchored the pages with her arms. It would just be the end if she let them drop into the water.

Geoff stepped close and looked at the drawings. "He said he put it all in the notes, just what he was looking for and what he needed help with. Are you sure you can do this?"

Josie glanced up, indignant.

Geoff's brow was wrinkled, and he ran his fingertips down his shirtfront.

Clarice took his arm. "You don't need to worry, Geoff. Josie *dreams* in numbers."

Josie shot Clarice a grateful look and carefully rolled the pages up again. "I'll get to work on these as soon as I get home. How should I contact you when I'm done?"

Geoff dug again into his pocket and produced a card. "Send word to me at this address when you're ready, and we'll arrange a time to meet."

Josie scanned the card, plain white with bold black lettering, nodding. Now that she had the plans, she itched to get started. How she wished her relationship with Eli wasn't so distant, having to go through someone else in order to share ideas and explore design possibilities. If only they could meet as equals, as peers in this project... But that was foolish. No powerful man like Eli would ever see her as a peer or respect her work and abilities enough to admit he needed her help. She glanced at her timepiece. "We'd best get back.

Mama will be wondering where we've gotten to."

"Oh no, not yet." Clarice's eyes implored Josie. "Just a few more minutes, please?"

Clarice had never been so open with Josie, had never let Josie see her want something so desperately. Pity again swamped Josie at their tangled situation.

"Here, before you have to go, there's something I wanted you to see." Geoff handed Josie a pair of field glasses from his pocket. "If you look over there"—he pointed across the harbor beyond the ore docks—"you can see the Kennebrae Shipyard. The ship you're working on is the *Bethany*."

Josie smiled and took the glasses. "Here, hang on to these while I walk up the way for a better look."

Geoff took the plans and the envelope back, giving Josie a grateful smile. "Take your time."

Josie walked toward the bridge, and when she was out of earshot of the couple, she lifted the binoculars. The great hulk of the *Bethany* swung into her view. Scaffolding shrouded her in a maze of boards and poles. The cleft amidships showed bright with new welds and repairs, ropes swung in the wind, and the deck had been removed like the lid of a sardine can. All that remained of the ship that had sat icebound just outside the harbor last winter was the hull and pilothouse and the great smokestack. Behind the ship, the long, sloped roof of the shipyard building loomed, KENNEBRAE SHIPPING painted in high, white letters on a vertical sign at the peak.

Resolve and eagerness merged as Josie scanned the length of the ship. She could do this. She *would* do this, for herself and for Eli. Though he may be out of her reach forever, she could still be joined with him in this project. They'd be unknowing partners in fulfilling his plans.

She lowered the glasses and looked over her shoulder. Clarice and Geoffrey had their heads together. Josie sighed. She'd best get back there and act the chaperone. The last thing any of them wanted was someone wondering why Clarice, engaged to a Kennebrae, would be out walking alone with another man.

She headed their direction, and as she neared, she realized that someone else was on an intercepting vector with the couple. The short, rounded man looked familiar to her, but she couldn't place him from that distance. She raised the glasses and brought his face close in her vision.

Uneasiness quickened her pulse and her steps. Where had she seen him before? He looked determined and purposeful. "Here." Josie put out her hand for the ship plans when she was close enough to Geoff. "We need to go, now."

"So soon?" He handed her the papers and frowned. A page fluttered away.

"Quick, catch it!" Josie hurried up the sidewalk after the sheet. Just as she bent down for it a shoe came down hard, sticking the page to the ground.

"Lose something?"

She looked up into the short man's face.

He took her elbow and helped her upright, then bent to retrieve the sheet. He looked at it, then at her, calculation gleaming in his eyes.

She took the page and folded it, tucking it in with the others rolled under her arm.

Geoffrey stalked up and nodded curtly. "Fox, what brings you down to the canal on a Sunday afternoon?"

"Wish it was the same reason as you. Hello, ladies. I don't believe we've met." Mr. Fox tipped his hat.

"The Misses Zahn. But they were just leaving."

Josie took the hint, settled the papers in her arms, and took Clarice's elbow. "I'll contact you as soon as I can about these."

eight

This was a bad idea, and it had taken Eli an entire week since speaking with Jonathan about courting to come up with even this much. What had possessed him to invite Clarice to the circus of all things? He sat in the Zahn parlor, rotating his hat brim in his hands.

Geoffrey would have a good laugh when he heard about that. Eli frowned. No, Geoff probably wouldn't laugh about it. Geoff didn't seem to laugh about anything these days.

The clock on the table beside him chimed the quarter hour. What was keeping Clarice?

A movement caught his eye. The curtains in the doorway swayed, and a pair of bright blue eyes peeked through the fringe edging. A black curl slipped off a shoulder, and a giggle erupted. More movement, scuffling, snickering, and two girls tumbled through the doorway onto the rug.

"You pushed me!" The smaller of the two scrambled up.

"Did not. You're just clumsy." The bigger girl stuck her tongue out at her little sister.

Eli said nothing. If there was anything that baffled him more than a woman, it was a little girl. The sisters seemed to suddenly remember his presence, for they lined up, shoulder to shoulder, and smoothed their aprons. They stared at him, the younger twisting one curl around her finger.

Mrs. Zahn sailed into the room.

Eli stood, grateful for an escape from the scrutiny.

"So sorry to keep you waiting, but it seems Clarice has succumbed to another of her sick headaches. She won't be able to accompany you on your outing." Her eyes had a hectic sheen, as if she were flustered but trying to hide it.

Relief rushed through his chest. Reprieve. "That's quite all right, madam. Please give her my regards." If he left now, he'd still have several hours to see to the laying of the first pieces of the loading system in the bottom of the hold. Not having to go to the circus felt more like shackles being dropped from his wrists.

"But I don't want to disappoint the girls. You see, Clarice promised them you'd take them in her stead." Mrs. Zahn cupped the back of the younger's head and pushed her forward a step. "They've talked of nothing else since breakfast. You will take them, won't you?"

He could have sworn the little girl's eyes filled with tears on command. How did she do that? The other one challenged him with her stare, unable to keep the excitement out of her eyes.

Before he could answer, Josie entered the room. She'd seemed levelheaded when he'd spoken to her at the wedding reception. When their eyes met, he couldn't seem to look away. What was it about her that intrigued him? The Zahn girls all looked cut from the same cloth, but something in her walk, in her expression, seemed so familiar to him and yet completely unknown.

He shrugged and forced himself to focus on what Mrs. Zahn was saying.

"They won't be any trouble. Josephine will go along and help you with them. And please, do accept my apologies for Clarice. She doesn't usually suffer from headaches."

Josie moistened her lips, and her right hand clasped the middle two fingers of her left hand and twisted them.

His attention was diverted by the littler one tugging on his coat sleeve. "You will take us, won't you? I want to see an elephant."

So Eli found himself in the center of a ruffled and beribboned tornado. High-pitched voices filled the airspace in the carriage, little bodies bounced on the seats, noticing everything. After less than three minutes, he gave up trying to follow the conversation and settled into his corner with crossed arms. How did he let himself get talked into this? His one goal of spending time with his intended had burst apart into this female cacophony. The closer they got to the circus tent, the more their excitement level grew.

Josie grabbed the smallest girl's waistband and pulled her back from where she tried to hang out the window. "Sit still, Giselle. You'll fall out on the road if you're not careful."

"But look at the flags. Look at the wagons."

Calliope music whistled and punctuated the air. Eli caught the scents of popcorn and sawdust and the musky smell of animals and canvas.

The Kennebrae coachman pulled the carriage up close to the big top and opened the door. Eli got out first to assist the girls. He needn't have bothered. They shot out like corks from a bottle, except for Josie. She took his hand and stepped down, not meeting his eyes. The wind blew a strand of hair across her cheek, and she hooked it back with her little finger, a gesture he remembered from the last time they'd spoken.

The barker beckoned them, and Antoinette grabbed his hand. "C'mon!" Her hair bounced as she wriggled and jumped.

He allowed himself to be led toward the open tent flap. "They sure are lively." He directed his comment over his shoulder to where Josie trailed behind. The little one had a tight grip on him, but he forced her to stop so he could dig in his pocket for enough change to buy four tickets. Josie stopped beside him, and he thought he caught a whiff of violets. "They seem to hop in all directions."

"You get used to it." She swallowed, and he found his attention centered on her delicate throat. "Thank you for taking us out today. I know you'd rather be with Clarice, and that Mama sort of cornered you into this. She can be quite forceful at times." A delicate flush brightened her cheeks, and her smoky lashes hid her eyes.

Would he? Would he rather be with Clarice? He had to admit no, not really. The little girls seemed eager for his company, where his fiancée avoided him to the point where it made her ill. And he found himself not reluctant to share Josie's company in particular. "Don't worry about it. You're never too old to see a circus."

They found seats on the hard benches, and Eli tried to maneuver them so he could sit by Josie, but he found himself between Antoinette and Giselle. Sharp elbows, enormous bows clipping him in the chin, and restless movement unsettled him. He looked over Giselle's head at Josie.

Her eyes moved, taking everything in. A band at the far end played a lively tune. "We've never been to the circus before." Her face, flushed with pleasure, attracted him.

"I'm glad you got to come then."

A man in a red-and-white-striped jacket and straw boater paused before their row. He carried a box suspended from his shoulders by wide straps. "Peanuts, popcorn, candy!"

Eli glanced down at Giselle, who had tucked her lips in and clasped her hands under her chin. It was the first time she'd sat still all day. Antoinette on his other side grinned at him with wide, hopeful eyes. With a chuckle and shrug, he dug into his breast pocket for his wallet. No sense going to the circus if you didn't eat some sweets.

Each girl selected her preference from the vendor. He noticed that Josie selected a striped bag of peppermint sticks, the least costly item offered. "Thank you, Mr. Kennebrae."

"Please, call me Eli, and it's my pleasure." And he found that it truly was. And that should bother him, shouldn't it? He had the distinct feeling that if Josie had been his fiancée and not the reluctant Clarice, he wouldn't mind the idea of matrimony in the least. His conscience jabbed him for his disloyal thoughts. But could a man be disloyal to a fiancée he'd neither sought nor wanted?

❧

Josie took another grip on her traitorous emotions. She shouldn't be enjoying this outing so much, not when she'd just finally decided to put Eli Kennebrae out of her mind and heart and pursue her mathematics. Not that it was the outing that caused her such turmoil. No, it was him.

The initial thrust of pleasure at seeing him again had subsided. In its wake, her heart beat fast against her ribs, her mouth went dry, and she couldn't seem to stop her eyes from straying in his direction every few seconds.

Poor Giselle. Josie had all but pushed her into the row before her so Josie wouldn't have to sit beside Eli. The little girl wriggled and gasped and talked nineteen to the dozen, masking Josie's emotional upheaval. At least she hoped it did.

"Balloons! Look at the balloons!" Giselle stood and pointed down where a white-faced clown with enormous checked pants walked past trailing a rainbow cloud of balloons.

Josie pressed her little sister's shoulder to get her to resume her seat. "Giselle, don't point. It's rude."

"But look at the funny man." She craned her neck and perched on the edge of the bench to follow him down the tent.

"Ladies and gentlemen, children of all ages!" The ringmaster bounded into the center ring, a bright light surrounding him and gleaming off his shiny high boots and tall hat.

Giselle's attention riveted on the red-coated man. Josie glanced out of the corner of her eye toward Eli. He appeared to be studying the poles and rigging overhead.

She allowed herself to be drawn into the spectacle, laughing at the clowns' antics, admiring the beautiful white horses and enormous elephants. The snarls of the tigers and lions made her skin prickle.

"And now, ladies and gentlemen, all the way from Budapest, I present to you the bravest, the most talented, the amazing Istvan Hrabowski!" The ringmaster made a sweeping gesture, and the spotlight shot upward to where a man stood on a tiny platform affixed to one of the tent poles. "Istvan, a magician of balance, a man who knows no fear, will dazzle you with his high-wire abilities! Thirty feet in the air, and no net should he fall. He risks death for your amusement."

Giselle pressed close to Josie. She pressed her lips against Josie's ear and whispered, "I'm scared. That man might fall."

Josie smoothed the girl's hair, not wanting to admit her own apprehension. She turned Giselle away from her and put her hands under the little girl's arms. "You can sit with me. And don't you worry. He's done this lots of times." At least she hoped he had.

Giselle snuggled close, hiding her eyes with her hands but peeking through her fingers. Josie suddenly realized that with Giselle in her lap, no one now sat between her and Eli.

He scooched along the bench toward her, his eyes clouded. "Is she all right?"

Josie nodded, touched by his concern. "It's a bit scary." She hugged Giselle close, taking comfort in the warm little body.

The performer, holding a long pole for balance, marched across the wire as casually as if he were walking down the street. The *rat-a-tat* of a drum accompanied him, echoing the beating of Josie's heart, intensifying her anxiety. Each trip he made across the taut cable, he added a level of difficulty. Each time he stepped safely onto the small platform, the band let out a flourish, and the man waved to the crowd, accepting their applause. Each time he started across with another apparatus, Josie sucked in her breath and held it.

When he started across with a chair in hand and placed it on the wire, she bit her lip, and Giselle tucked her head under Josie's chin. Eli slid a little closer, and somehow she found her hand clasped in his. Heat surged through her cheeks. Had she taken his hand, or had he taken hers?

He leaned close, his breath teasing her temple. "Don't be scared."

Josie forgot all about the man teetering dangerously overhead and concentrated on her heart teetering dangerously near to toppling over in her chest. This was wrong. Eli was Clarice's husband-to-be. No matter that he was only offering comfort, no matter that he hadn't shown the least inclination of affection for her, she shouldn't be holding his hand, and furthermore, she shouldn't be enjoying it so much. Her chest felt as if a dozen mice were scurrying around inside.

She didn't know who was more relieved when the Amazing Istvan navigated the wire for the last time, Giselle or herself. She disengaged her fingers from Eli's hand, already missing his touch but able to breathe easier after breaking contact. She couldn't look at him, instead lowering her chin to Giselle's shoulder so the little girl's head was between her and Eli.

The girls were much subdued on the ride home. Sated with sweets and popcorn, roasted peanuts and candy floss, they dragged into the carriage for the ride down the hill and across the canal. Josie kept Giselle in her lap and wasn't surprised when her two youngest sisters drifted into sleep. Antoinette's head rested against Eli's shoulder, and he smiled across the carriage at Josie.

She couldn't help responding to the warmth in his eyes. Her conscience elbowed her. He had been nothing but kind to them, a bachelor fettered with three girls on an outing. His handclasp had meant nothing more to him than if she had been Giselle. She should stop obsessing about it and try to remember he was her sister's fiancé.

nine

"You didn't even see her?" Grandfather pushed aside McKay's help and settled the lap robe across his thin legs himself. "I thought you had an outing planned."

Eli shrugged out of his jacket and draped it over the back of a chair. He yawned and loosened his tie. "I did, but she couldn't come. A headache, I believe." He had serious doubts about that headache.

"But you were gone all afternoon, and what's that smell?" Grandfather sniffed the air like a bird dog. "Is that popcorn?"

"Popcorn, peppermint, lemon drops, sawdust, and a dose of sarsaparilla. I spent the afternoon at the circus." He eased into the chair and rested his head against his jacket, breathing the scents in again. One scent lingered in his memory. Violets.

"The circus?"

"I tried to take Clarice but ended up taking her sisters instead."

McKay's normally impassive face twitched. He turned away and busied himself straightening things on Grandfather's desk. "Will that be all, sir?"

Grandfather waved the butler away. "Yes, yes, quit fussing. Go see if Melissa needs anything." He turned his attention back to Eli. "This is all your fault, you know."

"What's my fault?" Eli frowned and studied his fingernails.

"That things aren't progressing with Clarice. There's no reason why you two can't make a sensible, suitable match. I did my homework. Her family is respectable. She's even tempered and more than passably good-looking." Grandfather picked up the letter opener on his desk and rotated the point against his palm. "Radcliffe came by this morning and said he's not happy with how this engagement is going. He's concerned that you're not spending enough time with the girl. And I agree."

"What do you want me to do? I made the offer. She couldn't come. Or wouldn't come." He had to admit he wasn't used to women avoiding him. Though he hadn't ever courted before, he never assumed it would be so hard. How could he court a girl he couldn't get near?

"You're not doing anything to further this relationship. The circus? How childish is that? If you want to win this girl—and more importantly, win her father's approval again—you've got to do something romantic for her. Flowers, candy, that sort of thing. When I courted your grandmother—God rest her soul—she expected flowers every time I visited. . .and the occasional drive in the country and sweets. And Jonathan brings Melissa roses for everything. You saw the bouquets after Matthew was born."

Flowers. He could do that. Get McKay to send a bunch or two. And the confectioner's shop delivered. "And that will get you off my back? I have work to do. She should understand that I can't be spending every waking minute trying to figure out what will make her happy." He rose, his muscles tight in annoyance. "I don't know why I have to court the girl anyway. We're already engaged, thanks to you. Seems we bypassed courting some time back."

The letter opener clattered to the desk. "You'll court the girl because it's the gentlemanly thing to do and because her father wishes it. Also because I wish it, and I'm footing the bride price by financing your shipbuilding schemes."

Eli bit back the hot retort burning his tongue. He couldn't afford to get Grandfather so riled he withdrew the money. "Any other suggestions?" If his lips got any stiffer, they might snap right off.

"It's high time you bought the engagement ring. Jewelry

always works on a woman. Get her something you know she'll like, something big and sparkly that shows you spent some time and a considerable amount of cash. That will turn her head in your direction and mollify her mother at the same time."

"I don't know anything about jewelry shopping. And I've no clue what she would like." At the idea of walking into a jewelry store and picking out a ring, his heart quailed. It was too much to ask. "Couldn't she just go pick something out herself and charge it to my account?"

"You don't know a blessed thing about women."

"That's what I've tried to tell you. You're the one who backed me into this corner. If I had my way, I'd still be a happily oblivious bachelor who had nothing more complex to think about than what gauge steel to use for the new beams in the cargo hold of the *Bethany*. I couldn't begin to imagine what kind of engagement ring to buy for Clarice Zahn." Just saying the words made his skin crawl. All this was getting uncomfortably close to real and harder to push to the back of his mind. He wanted to concentrate on his ship, not on this stupid engagement.

"I raised you smarter than that. If you want to know what she likes, then ask her. Or better yet, ask her mother. But get it done." Grandfather rang the bell for McKay. "I can't do everything for you."

The butler entered so quickly, Eli suspected he had hovered in the hall. McKay shot him an inquiring glance, but Eli shrugged.

"He didn't want you. I did." Grandfather tugged on the wheels of his invalid chair. "I have to do everything around here. Send a note to Pearson's Jewelers that this stubborn grandson of mine will be in tomorrow afternoon to purchase an engagement ring. Tell them to have the best in the store ready for him and a private room for viewing."

"Tomorrow? I can't tomorrow. I'm meeting with my job foreman all afternoon."

"No, you're not. You're meeting with the jeweler. Find out what the girl likes and get a ring on her hand as soon as possible."

❦

Josie hid in the library, trying to concentrate on mathematics and forget the happiness of being in Eli's presence all yesterday afternoon.

Clarice hadn't been the least bit interested in hearing about the circus, and it wasn't until much later last night she confessed that Geoffrey had met her in the garden while Josie was uptown. Her sister's eyes glowed, and she kept sighing and staring off into the distance. Her only response when Josie mentioned Eli was to brush aside the comment. "Don't worry about it. Geoffrey says he has a plan."

Josie didn't know what to do. On the one hand, her heart broke for Clarice, forced to marry one man when her heart clearly belonged to Geoffrey. But what about Eli? He didn't deserve such shoddy treatment from his fiancée. Why, if anyone found out about Geoffrey and Clarice's clandestine meeting, Clarice would be ruined, Geoffrey would be fired, and Eli would be humiliated. Geoffrey may have a plan, but it was only a delay tactic, keeping Eli focused on his ship. Eventually Mama would set a wedding date and expect Clarice to say her vows. What a mess. Josie had escaped to the library as soon as she could to try to get a hold on her emotions.

"Miss Josie, there's a gentleman here to see you." The housekeeper entered the library and handed Josie a calling card.

Her heart rocketed into high gear. Mr. Eli Kennebrae. "Are you sure this is for me? Isn't he here to see Clarice?" She casually turned over the paper she was working on in her lap, hiding the drawing.

"He asked for you." The spare, stern woman folded her weathered hands at the waist of her immaculate white apron. "Shall I tell him you're at home?"

Josie swung her feet down from the chair and straightened. "Show him to the parlor. I'll be there in a minute." Her mind raced. What could he want? She had to stand on tiptoe to see her reflection in the mirror over the desk. Traitorous color bloomed on her cheekbones. She smoothed her hair up into its loose bun and checked her dress was straight. Just before she left the library she tucked her books and papers away. It wouldn't do to leave them lying around where anyone could see them.

He stood near the front window, Mama's Boston fern almost touching his black pant leg. His hands clasped behind him, he didn't see her at first. She took a moment to notice how his brown hair swept back from his intelligent brow and how the strong column of his neck, suntanned and smooth, disappeared into his snowy collar.

Josie cleared her throat softly. His head came around, and she stared into his eyes. For a long moment, neither moved. All the warm feelings she'd been shoving down about him welled up and threatened to spill out of her gaze. She quickly lowered her eyelashes and schooled her features to be polite but distant. Why was it she could still feel the clasp of his fingers around hers? *Stop it. Concentrate or you'll say something stupid and embarrass yourself.*

"Josie." His smile brightened his face. "Thank you for seeing me. I have a tremendous favor to ask of you. Would you be so kind as to accompany me downtown this afternoon?"

He took her breath away. He was asking her? She tried to retrieve some air while her mind galloped as fast as her heart. What about Clarice? Was this proper? "Are you sure you don't want my sister?" Perhaps he had done what many people did and confused her for one of her siblings. There were a lot of Zahn girls.

His lips twitched. "I assure you I don't wish to see any other of your siblings. I have need of your expertise."

His words shot through her like a bolt. "My expertise?" Had Geoffrey spilled the beans about her math abilities?

"I find myself in the unfamiliar position of purchasing an engagement ring. I had hoped you would go to the jeweler's and assist me in choosing one your sister would like." He shook his head. "Grandfather suggested I ask your mother to help me, but I'd much prefer your aid. Surely you know your sister's tastes and could advise me."

Josie instantly knew the meaning of the word *bleak*. Was God testing her resolve?

At her hesitation, his gaze sharpened. "Have I stepped out of line? I suppose I assumed now would be all right. The jeweler is expecting me in about half an hour."

"No, not at all." Josie clamped down on her emotions and strove to be polite. "I'll just get my hat and gloves."

Josie practiced rigid self-control on the ride. She answered Eli politely when he commented about the weather and the ship lying at anchor just outside the harbor awaiting entrance to load tons of iron at the ore docks. She remembered to thank him again for taking her and her sisters to the circus.

He seemed to swallow up all the air in the carriage, though he sat across from her and didn't crowd her legs. "I hope it wasn't too stimulating for Giselle. I've never seen anyone sleep so soundly as she did on the ride home."

"She's talked of nothing else since." Josie smiled fondly, remembering how Giselle had clasped her hands round the bedpost and swung back and forth as she talked. "You made quite an impression on Giselle and Antoinette. I suspect both girls are nursing a bit of puppy love now." Not to mention herself and the silly infatuation she cherished for him that refused to die no matter how often she tried to strangle it.

He laughed. "Only Giselle and Antoinette? And here I thought I'd cast my net wider. And where did all those French names come from? Zahn's not French."

"No, Zahn is actually German." She grimaced. "The French names were Mama's idea, one that Papa regrets intensely. She thought it made us sound more aristocratic."

Eli shrugged in sympathy. "I'm told my mother insisted on Bible names for her sons. Jonathan and Noah are all right names, but Eli? Who wants to be named after a man who was such a dismal failure as a priest and as a father?"

"You shouldn't look at it that way. Look at his good qualities. He recognized the call of God on Samuel's life, and he raised Samuel right. Eli's a fine name." Josie didn't know why she felt the need to defend his name. It shouldn't matter to her if he liked his mother's choice or not.

The carriage rocked to a stop. Eli hopped out and helped her down before the coachman could. "Thank you for coming with me today. I confess I don't have the faintest idea what your sister might like."

Regret, jealousy, a bit of disgruntlement? Josie couldn't identify the emotions bouncing around inside her. This excursion would be so different if he was buying a ring for her. A hush descended the moment her foot touched the plush carpeting. Bright gaslights shone powerful beams down on display cases of dazzling jewels. Lighted alcoves of gleaming silver service and flatware marched down the walls of the shop.

"Mr. Kennebrae? I'm Marlow Pearson, the proprietor." A corpulent man with a jolly face came toward them. His quiet voice seemed in contrast to the smile he directed. Short arms barely reached across his middle, and his neck and several chins spilled out over the top of his collar. "And this is your young lady? Splendid."

Josie looked quickly at Eli's face then dropped her gaze to her hemline.

Eli shook the fat fingers offered to him and said, "This is Miss Zahn. She's come to help me choose just the right ring."

Josie looked up again. Why hadn't he bothered to correct the jeweler? And why did it feel nice to be considered his young lady?

"Right this way. I've laid out a selection for you, but if they don't suffice, let me know." Mr. Pearson's short legs rolled under his bulk, but his feet made no sound as he led them toward the back of the shop. A door that at first glance seemed part of the rich walnut paneling opened at his touch, revealing a small conference room.

"Please, have a seat." Mr. Pearson opened a heavy felt cloth and spread it on the gleaming tabletop. From a cart along the wall, he produced a tray of black velvet, studded with rings. "I'll just turn up the lights a bit, so you can see them better." He turned the key on the overhead lamp to increase the flame.

Eli held Josie's chair then sat beside her.

Josie couldn't take her eyes off those rings. Diamonds in every shape and arrangement, some big as gravel. Rubies, sapphires, emeralds, and more diamonds. They must be worth a king's ransom.

"See anything you like?" Eli leaned back as if he had no interest in the proceedings.

Pearson hovered, rubbing his fingertips with his thumbs. Probably already counting the profits to be made from her choice. So many rings to choose from. Not a single space on the tray remained empty. Having the proprietor looming like a gargoyle on a cornice didn't help. He seemed to sense her hesitation. "Let me get you some coffee or tea. It's a big decision, picking out a ring. Take your time."

As soon as the door closed silently behind the round little man, Josie turned to Eli. "These stones are huge. Are you sure?"

"You think she won't like one of them? Grandfather seemed to think the bigger the better when it came to precious stones."

"Clarice does like diamonds, and I know Mama would love for her to have a real showpiece to brag about."

"But you don't?" His attention focused on her face.

She shrugged. "This isn't about what I want. This is about Clarice." She wasn't sure if she said it to remind him or to remind herself.

"Well, suppose it was about what you wanted. What would you choose, and how would it differ from what Clarice would like?" He sat up and leaned on his crossed arms on the edge of the table.

She surveyed the engagement rings again. "I suppose I'd choose this one, if it was for me." An oval stone that shot rainbows of turquoise and magenta in tiny sparkles mingled with gold. An opal. The smallest, plainest ring in the collection.

His eyebrows shot up. "Not a diamond?" He seemed puzzled by her choice but not displeased.

"Diamonds always seem so cold to me. Opals seem alive. Look at how it shimmers in the light. At first glance, unimpressive, but when you get to know it, when you bother to take a closer look, the real beauty comes through. Diamonds all look alike. No two opals are ever the same."

Mr. Pearson elbowed the door open, holding a tray of coffee. When he saw her holding the opal ring, he set the tray down and held out his hand. "I see you found the ring I included to gauge size. That really isn't an engagement ring, certainly not one suitable for the bride of Eli Kennebrae."

Josie's fingers closed over the ring, reluctant to let it go.

Eli took her hand and opened her chilly fingers. "Try it on. Might as well see what size would be best, right?"

Her mouth went dry as an attic floor. He slid the ring over her finger. She couldn't meet his eyes. The opal shimmered, a perfect fit. Her voice deserted her. Perhaps it was the enormous lump lodged in her throat.

"An excellent omen." Mr. Pearson beamed. "Now that we know the size, perhaps you'd like to try on one of the engagement rings."

Tears smarted Josie's eyes, and she had to force herself to remove the ring and concentrate on her real task for being there. When she could trust herself to speak, she swallowed hard and pointed to an emerald-cut diamond surrounded by smaller diamonds. "This one, I think. And the size is close enough."

At the broad smile that wreathed Mr. Pearson's face, she supposed her choice must've been among the most expensive rings on offer. She couldn't stand it anymore and pushed her chair away from the table. "I believe I'll wait out in the showroom."

Once in the serenity of the showroom, she paused beside a case of gold and silver watches to catch her breath. She hoped Clarice would like her choice. It wasn't Clarice's fault. And Mama would definitely approve the ring.

A shop assistant watched her but didn't approach.

Eli and Mr. Pearson emerged from the back room, shook hands, and parted.

"Thank you, Mr. Kennebrae. A pleasure doing business with you. And don't forget, we have wedding rings and pearl necklaces as well. Pearls would make an excellent wedding gift for your bride."

Josie slipped out the door before she had to hear anymore.

ten

Eli pored over the calculations, his first installment from Professor Josephson. He had to admit the mathematics looked sound. Page after page of neat drawings in a legible hand. Suggestions for improvements to his original designs that stirred Eli's imagination and caused new ideas to mushroom in his mind.

"Sir?"

He looked up, tugging his mind away from his designs. His foreman stood in the doorway of the shack Eli had purloined at the shipyard for his on-site office. "Yes, Gates?"

"Sir, the steel that came in for the bulkhead supports. . ." Gates rubbed his hands along his sides and looked anywhere but at Eli.

Dread settled into his heart. What could go wrong now? One thing after another had delayed the project.

"The steel is four inches too long. We'll have to cut it down before we can install it."

Relief trickled through Eli's chest. "Too long is better than too short. How long will it take to trim it to fit?"

"A day at least."

"Our launch date is getting later and later. At this rate, the harbor will be iced in before we're finished."

"Yes, sir." Gates hovered, mangling his hat brim with his gnarled fingers. "And, sir?"

"What is it now?" Eli tucked his papers into his attaché case. He'd get no more work done here today.

"The men, sir. They've heard that Keystone Steel is hiring shipbuilders and paying a dollar a day more than Kennebrae's."

"A dollar more a day?"

Gates nodded and scratched the hair over his left ear. "A dollar more a day for general labor. Welders and crane operators get two dollars more per day."

Eli had the distinct feeling Gates wasn't finished. "And what about yard foremen? Is Gervase Fox looking for one of those, too?"

Gates studied the rafters of the lean-to. "Yes, sir, he is. One of his men met me on my way out of the shipyard last night. Said he could offer me double wages and a fifty-dollar bonus just for signing on with Keystone."

"How many have jumped ship so far?" Without workers, he'd never get this ship finished. How like Fox. Couldn't buy the plans, couldn't buy Eli, so he tried to buy Eli's workers.

"Nobody so far, but the men are talking. They sent me in here to negotiate for them."

A heavy weight pressed on Eli's shoulders. The last thing he needed was a workforce problem. But would Grandfather turn loose enough money to increase the payroll by that much? He'd have to risk it.

"Tell the men I'll match the offer from Keystone. And for you, too. But tell them I expect value for my money. This ship will be completed by the original deadline and according to the specifications I've laid out." Eli stared hard at Gates. "I'll expect you to handle the men. Do whatever it takes to keep them on task. At that kind of money, they should meet the deadlines I set for them."

Gates nodded, smiling. "I'll tell them, sir. They'll be glad to hear it."

Eli picked up his case and followed his foreman into the sunshine. He wished he thought Grandfather would be glad to hear it. At least the sun was shining. Four days of heavy rain and lightning had kept the crews off the refit. Iron clanked, sparks flew, and men shouted. The dank, muddy smell of the harbor mingled with the odor of smoke and oil.

Before he could leave the shipyard, three more small problems arose. It seemed for each step he made forward on the project, the details and irritants dragged him back five. If he wasn't dealing with personnel issues, it was supply or weather or finances. Were all projects as fraught with setbacks as this one?

The carriage ride to the shipping office barely gave him time to marshal his thoughts. He was still juggling papers and ideas as he mounted the marble steps to the second-floor conference room. He'd come to dread these weekly reports to Grandfather and Jonathan. If he had good news about the ship, they dogged him about his engagement. When he had some good news to report on that front—though he had to admit that hadn't happened often—they grilled him about progress on the *Bethany*.

They were waiting when he arrived five minutes late. He took his customary seat where he wouldn't have to look at Grandfather's portrait and he wouldn't have to look directly at Grandfather himself.

"Glad you could make it. Are you sure we're not imposing on your schedule?" Grandfather rapped the edge of the table.

Eli blew out his breath and reached for his papers. He could practically see the purse strings tightening.

Jonathan rolled a pencil between his palms, the soft clicking as it rolled over his wedding band rhythmic and somehow comforting. Jonathan had a way with Grandfather. Of course, he'd been the number-one grandson for years, and not just because he was the eldest but because he loved Kennebrae Shipping with a passion that rivaled Grandfather's. The fact that Jonathan's wife had produced an heir to the Kennebrae dynasty had further put him in Grandfather's good graces.

The meeting went far worse than Eli had imagined. Grandfather stormed at the delays, raged at the increase in wages, and scoffed at Eli's reasoning. Eli should've known better than to mention Professor Josephson.

"You've never met the man? You didn't review his credentials?" Grandfather smacked the arm of his chair. "Yet you're willing to hang the entire project on his so-called expertise. And not only this project but the reputation of Kennebrae Shipping."

Eli's temper raised its head. "Yes. Yes, I am. The calculations are sound, and your reputation is in no danger. The only smear on your good name would be if word got out that Gervase Fox had stolen your workforce through higher wages."

"Fox? Fox is the one behind this wage hike?"

"That's right. He offered substantial raises to any Kennebrae shipyard worker willing to leave us and go to work for him."

Grandfather's eyes glittered with an emotion Eli feared was hate. Certainly animosity. "We'll see about that. I'll authorize the wage increase, and I'll see about Fox."

"Now, don't go off half-cocked." Jonathan looked up from his notes. "You might not like Fox—I can't say that I do either—but don't let him goad you into doing something foolish because you can't separate business from personal feelings."

Grandfather's lips twitched, and he fingered the blanket in his lap. "Don't patronize me. I was dealing with varmints like Gervase Fox when you were still in short pants." He turned his attention back to Eli. "What else do you have to report?"

"That's all."

"That's all? What about Clarice? Did she like the ring?"

Rocking back in his chair, Eli winced. "I haven't given it to her yet."

"I have had it with your delays. Do I have to do everything? You get that ring on her finger before dinnertime or you can kiss this project good-bye. In fact, I'll go along with you, just to make sure you do the thing up right. I'd like a word with Radcliffe anyway."

"Can't you trust me to get the job done by myself? I'm not a child, you know."

"There have been enough delays. I want this union signed and sealed and the Zahn lumber shipping contracts firmly in our pockets."

Eli winced at the mercenary gleam in Grandfather's eye.

Jonathan frowned at his papers. "You don't have to do this, Eli."

"Jonathan"—Grandfather held up his hand—"don't horn in here."

"I have to. Did you learn nothing from what you did to me and what you did to Noah? I can't stand by and let you shove Eli into a marriage he doesn't want to a girl he doesn't know, all for profit of a company that doesn't need the help. Kennebrae Shipping is bursting at the seams with orders and contracts. The Zahn lumber, though it would be nice, shouldn't be bought at the expense of Eli's freedom. I have a feeling you're more interested in keeping the contract away from Gervase Fox than you are about getting it for yourself."

"Your marriage and Noah's are the best things to ever happen to you boys, and you know it. Who's to say it won't be the same for Eli? I'm not a fool. Do you think I don't know my own grandsons? Did you think I didn't have these girls checked out thoroughly? I made wise choices for you all. It isn't my fault you both took the long way around to finding happiness. I intend for Eli to take a direct course. Get the ring on her finger and get her to the altar. He'll thank me later."

"I can't tell you how enjoyable it is to be discussed as if I wasn't sitting right here." Eli stared at his brother and grandfather, twisting his mouth wryly. "Jonathan, I appreciate the effort, but I have to see this through. As Grandfather's so proud of saying, once a Kennebrae gives his word, he follows through."

Grandfather almost purred in satisfaction on the way to the elevator.

Eli pushed Grandfather's chair through the lobby and toward the brass and glass front doors. When they were seated in Grandfather's carriage, Eli patted the ring in his pocket. In a long day of nothing going right, he hoped that this at least would be done to Grandfather's satisfaction. Eli certainly found no satisfaction in the idea, and from the skittish way Clarice behaved around him, he thought she might not either.

☙

Mama's wails could shatter glass. Josie sat in shock beside Grandma Bess, who flipped pages in the latest *Saturday Evening Post*, occasionally looking up to consider her daughter-in-law's hysterics.

Mama clutched her handkerchief and every so often picked up the piece of paper in her lap and scanned it again. "How could she do this to me? What will I tell Radcliffe? And you, Josephine, can explain to him just what your role in this catastrophe is. It's plain as a pineapple you had something to do with this." Mama waved the paper again.

The soft chime of the doorbell galvanized Josie. She rose, grateful for a valid reason to leave the room. Footsteps clattered on the upstairs hall, followed by a high-pitched little-girl giggle. Through the shirred curtain covering the oval of glass in the oak door, she could make out a man's shadow, tall with a hat.

She opened the door and froze stiff as an icicle.

Eli swept his hat from his head and smoothed his hair.

Josie opened her mouth but couldn't think of a thing to say.

Next to Eli on the porch, Abraham Kennebrae sat in his chair, his thin hands in his lap, his black suit and white shirt immaculate.

"Who is it, Josephine?" Mama seemed to have forgotten

her manners completely, screeching the question from the front parlor.

Josie blinked, making sure she wasn't seeing things, then shrugged. "It's the Kennebraes," she called over her shoulder, still looking at Eli from the corner of her eye while she spoke.

Josie winced at the wail that followed. When she heard a soft thump, her heart tripled its pace. She rushed to the parlor, leaving their callers standing on the front porch. Mama had fainted.

Grandma Bess took control in the same calm manner in which she did everything.

Eli helped lift Mama onto the couch. Her head lolled back and one arm hung over the side of the sofa and trailed the floor. He stepped back, eyebrows high, but asked no questions.

Josie tried to meld into the alcove beside the Boston fern.

Grandma dug in her enormous bag and produced a small vial of smelling salts. "Octavia, wake up. Pull yourself together and stop giving in to these histrionics. You'd think the world had come crashing to an end." Grandma waved the little bottle under Mama's nose.

The pungent odor worked, for Mama's eyes shot open and she began to cough. Eli and Grandma helped her sit up. Mama clasped her chest, gasping for air, took one look at Eli, and wailed again.

"Madam, please." Abraham Kennebrae wheeled his chair closer. "Do we need to call a doctor? Or perhaps your husband? Is Radcliffe at home?"

Mention of Papa stopped Mama's cries like slamming a door. She snatched the handkerchief Grandma offered and dabbed her eyes and upper lip.

Eli stooped to pick up a piece of paper from the floor, and when Mama would've snatched it away, Grandma swatted her hand. "Let the young man read it. It concerns him more than you."

Eli scanned the page, but Mr. Kennebrae jabbed him in the side. "Read it aloud, boy."

"Dear Mama and Papa,
By now you know I've gone. I tried to stay, to do what you wished of me, but I just can't. You see, my heart belongs to another, and I could never be happy as Eli Kennebrae's bride. I do wish you'd have told me your plans before involving Mr. Kennebrae. He's a very nice man, but not for me. By the time you read this note, I will be married. I've eloped with my true love, Geoffrey Fordham. Please don't worry about me, and please tell Josie thanks for everything. Without her, I wouldn't have had the courage to do this.

Love,
Mrs. Geoffrey Fordham."

A hollow ache filled Josie for Eli. How did he keep his voice so calm, like he was reading about strangers instead of his fiancée and his good friend? She supposed Clarice couldn't resist the urge to sign her married name, but that had to hurt Eli. When she glanced over at him, his face merely looked thoughtful and detached.

His grandfather looked anything but disinterested. He snatched the paper from Eli's hand and read it himself. The spidery blue veins stood out on his hands and his fingers shook, while a dull red crept up from his celluloid collar and spread to his cheeks. Josie thought Mama might faint again when his black, burning eyes bored into her.

Before he could say anything, Papa walked through the front doorway. He strolled into view through the parlor doorway, newspaper tucked under his arm, hat set at a jaunty angle. He tapped his walking stick a couple of times on the rug, then tossed it in the air and caught it before sliding it into the hall tree with a flourish. When he spied the crowd in the parlor, his eyebrows shot up. "Kennebrae, good to see you. Beautiful day out, isn't it? Stay for supper, won't you?"

Instead of answering, Mr. Kennebrae handed Papa Clarice's note. Josie held her breath. Papa's jovial expression vanished, as if someone had wiped a hand down his face. In its place, shock, disbelief, and anger cycled through. The last lingered. Josie expected a reaction like a boiler explosion, but Papa's words came out in a tight whisper. "Mother, go see to dinner. Abraham, Eli, Octavia, let us retire to my library to confer over this matter."

Mama walked as if she couldn't feel her feet on the carpet, lifting her legs high and coming down with more force than usual, and Father followed her.

Eli put his hands on the back of Mr. Kennebrae's chair. To Josie's surprise, a smile lifted the corners of Eli's mouth once he was out of sight of his grandfather. He caught her looking at him and shrugged.

Now what was she to make of that?

eleven

Eli had to restrain himself from laughing out loud. No wonder Geoffrey had been so touchy about Eli's engagement to Clarice. He'd been in love with her all along. A condemned man escaping the hangman's noose couldn't have felt more elation than Eli did at that moment.

The scowl on Grandfather's features told him he'd better keep that elation to himself. He figured he could just about fry an egg on the top of Grandfather's head, the old man was so angry.

As soon as the library doors shut behind them, Grandfather started in. "Radcliffe, what's the meaning of this? My grandson comes over here in good faith to put a ring—a very expensive ring, mind you—on your daughter's finger, and what do we find? She's eloped!" He pounded the arm of his chair with one hand in a familiar gesture.

Zahn rocked back on his heels at this attack and glared at Abraham. "With *your* lawyer, I might add." He shifted his eyes to include Eli in his displeasure. "Did you put him up to it?"

"No, sir." Eli's lips twitched. "They did this all on their own. I had no idea Geoff had feelings for your daughter. If I had known, there's no way I would've gone along with this engagement. I don't poach on another man's preserve." He shoved his hands in his pockets and leaned against a bookcase.

Mrs. Zahn collapsed into a chair near the fireplace, her feet shooting out and kicking a pile of papers and books on the cold hearth. She seemed not to notice the mess she'd made, fanning herself with her handkerchief and staring into space. "What was she thinking? She'll be ruined, that's what. Running off to get married, and when she was engaged to another man." The lady hiccupped and blinked, choking on the words.

"When did you first notice she was gone?" Zahn fired the question at his wife. "Perhaps it isn't too late to fetch her back."

For a moment hope dawned on her rounded face. Then her shoulders slumped and her eyelids fell. "I found the note this afternoon when I was getting ready to leave for Mrs. Grant's garden party. I don't know how I missed seeing it all day. Clarice wasn't at breakfast this morning, but you know how she is." Mrs. Zahn put her chin up defensively. "She rarely eats breakfast anyway, so I didn't miss her. I couldn't have known she'd do something like this. No one here has seen her since yesterday after the evening meal. She's probably been gone since last night."

Zahn paced the rug, his brows down like a thundercloud, his steps rigid.

Grandfather tugged on Eli's sleeve. "Well, don't just stand there like a lamppost. What are you going to do about this?"

"Me?" Eli shrugged. "I'm not going to do anything. I'm the wronged party here, remember?"

Zahn stopped mid-stride. Inspiration lifted his features from hard, etched lines to something resembling his expression when he first entered the house. "I've got it." His fingers snapped like a gunshot and brought Mrs. Zahn upright in her chair.

"What?" Grandfather hunched his shoulders and leaned forward.

"A Kennebrae-Zahn wedding." Zahn looked as if the ideas tumbling in his head were all falling into logical order. "Of course. Just because Clarice isn't here doesn't mean we can't go ahead with a wedding. There's the next one in line." He snapped his fingers again and looked to his wife.

"Josephine?"

"Yes, that's it." He turned to Eli. "You can marry Josephine."

Eli's thoughts boggled. The man couldn't even remember his daughter's name and here he was swapping one for another like a new tie or pair of gloves. "You're not serious."

"Of course I am." He seemed puzzled at the statement. "It's the perfect solution."

"No, it isn't." Eli shook his head. Had Zahn lost his wits?

Grandfather turned his chair. "Radcliffe, I'd like a few moments alone with my grandson, if you please."

Eli braced himself for whatever Grandfather would say. He took his hands out of his pockets and straightened away from the bookcase. Grandfather barely waited for the Zahns to leave before going on the attack. "This is all your fault."

"Excuse me?"

"If you'd put more of an effort into courting the girl, she wouldn't have eloped with Fordham. Who, by the way, will never work for Kennebrae's again."

Eli shrugged. "I think it took a lot of courage for Geoffrey to do this, and Clarice, too. Though I wish they would've come to me. I'd have released her from the engagement and given them my blessing."

"And lost yourself the *Bethany* in the process!" Grandfather's voice and color rose. "We had a deal."

Eli's anger charged forward to meet Grandfather's. "A deal I no longer want any part of. It's choked me for weeks. I'm not willing to exchange my freedom for a ship or money. I wanted to make my mark on Kennebrae Shipping, but the cost is too great. You can keep the *Bethany*. I'll take my designs elsewhere. It isn't as if I haven't had other offers. You've manipulated me for long enough. Working for Fox couldn't be as bad as being stretched on the rack by you every day."

"You wouldn't leave."

"Watch me." Eli started for the door, intent on putting a lot of distance between him and his conniving grandsire. He was free, released from his obligations, and it felt great.

"Eli, please." The plea stopped him in his tracks. Grandfather sounded broken and defeated. "I want you to do this. . . for me." Grandfather picked up Clarice's letter from the corner of the desk and creased it with his thumbnail.

Frustration at his inability to just walk away from the old man made Eli's voice raspy. "Why? Why is it so important to you that I get married right now? Why can't you be happy that Jonathan and Noah are married and let me get on with my own life?"

"Because I gave my word."

"It doesn't matter now. Don't you see? *You* tried to keep your word. *I* tried to keep your word, but the girl has flown the coop. No one will blame you for not following through this time. It's impossible now that she's married. Zahn can't hold us to the bargain." Eli sank onto the window seat so that he was at eye level with Grandfather. "I'm sorry about the shipping contracts, but maybe you can still work something out with him."

"This isn't about Zahn. It never was." Grandfather scowled.

"Suppose you tell me then just what this *is* about."

Grandfather pinched the bridge of his nose and rested his elbows on the arms of his chair. He stared past Eli's shoulder for a long moment then breathed deeply, as if coming to a decision. "I promised your grandmother—God rest her soul—on her deathbed that I would see you boys all safely married to good girls before I died. I gave my word to her." He spoke the last phrase slowly, as if to emphasize just what it meant to him. "And I'm running out of time."

"You're not that old. You're going to live on for years yet. Look at how not even a stroke has slowed you down much. I plan to get married eventually. Why can't you wait until then?" Eli kept his hand on the doorknob, wary of another of Grandfather's traps.

"Time's always shorter than you think, and mine's dwindling fast." His words caused Eli to turn around. "The doc gave me the long face a year ago, said I'd best be making my final plans. That's why I've been after you boys to marry quickly. I promised your grandmother, and I aim to keep my word before it's too late."

"The long face?"

"It's something with my heart. The doc says I could go at any time."

"Your heart?" His mind refused to accept it. Life without his recalcitrant and calculating grandfather? Impossible.

"Help me, Eli. Help a Kennebrae keep his word to his own."

The noose Eli had so easily slipped out of only a short while before dropped over his head and tightened.

⁂

Josie bolted up the stairs to change for dinner. The turmoil of this afternoon's events sent her thoughts tumbling.

Wild giggles emanated from her bedroom. She opened the door to see Giselle and Antoinette wearing her two best gowns and her widest-brimmed afternoon hats.

"Girls!"

They stopped pirouetting in front of the armoire mirror and looked up at her with wide blue eyes. Toni had tried to pin up her black tresses, and one long sausage curl escaped and bounced along her cheek.

"Hand it over." Josie held out her palm.

Giselle gave her the ivory fan she'd been fluttering under her chin and began to peel off the satin gloves.

"You, too." Josie waited for Toni.

The girls shed the dresses and necklaces, the hats and scarves.

"And put them away where you got them." Josie was inclined

to indulge them. After all, what harm had they done? It brought back memories of a small Josie and Clarice invading Grandma Bess's bureau and trunk and trying on treasures.

The indulgence Josie felt evaporated the moment she saw her desk. "You little horrors, look what you've done!" An avalanche of papers and books had slid off the desk into a heap on the floor. Her carefully arranged drawings were under the desk, and the papers she'd intended to burn were mingled with the ones she needed to keep. "How many times do I have to tell you to keep your little paddies off my stuff?" She clapped her hands onto her hips and glared at her sisters.

Giselle's lower lip began to quiver, and water formed on her lashes. "Josie, we're sorry. We didn't mean to." The rose-colored satin and lace of Josie's best dress drooped off Giselle's narrow shoulders, and the skirts puddled around her on the floor.

Josie caved. "I'm sorry, girls. I know you didn't mean to, but you have to stay out of my things. If you'd have asked me, I'd have let you play dress-up. I have some very important papers in here that can't get messed up."

The tears released from Giselle's lower lashes and tracked down her pale cheeks. She sniffed and nodded, the ostrich feather on Josie's hat bobbing with the movement.

Toni shucked Josie's second-best dress and opened the armoire door. "We won't do it again, Josie. And we'll help you clean up."

"Good, because we're having guests for dinner, and I have to get ready."

With the help of her sisters, Josie got the mess cleaned up. "Here, Toni, these are the ones I'm done with. Put them in this envelope, and I'll throw them in the fire later." She held out the large brown envelope Geoffrey had sent, and Toni slid the much-scribbled pages and notes inside.

Josie hurriedly scrubbed her hands, scowling at an ink

smear that wouldn't budge. Still, no one would be looking at her hands, not with the uproar Clarice's elopement had caused. With trepidation, she descended the stairs and entered the parlor.

Papa and Eli rose as she came in.

Mama popped up out of her chair and came toward Josie, smiles wreathing her face, her eyes suspiciously bright. "Here she is, and doesn't she look a picture?" Mama clasped Josie's hands, kissed the air beside her cheek, and whispered, "What took you so long?"

Josie glanced at Eli, who resumed his seat and stared at his hands. Worry lines wrinkled his forehead, and the relieved grin he'd worn the last time she saw him had vanished. Perhaps the reality of losing Clarice was beginning to set in. Josie's heart went out to him, and she wondered why he had agreed to stay to dinner. When they entered the dining room, he sat in the chair normally reserved for Clarice, and Josie took her customary spot in the next seat.

Grandma Bess's mouth looked pinched, as if she wanted to say something but refrained. And the way Mama avoided looking at Grandma made Josie wonder if verbal swords hadn't already been crossed. Mama kept the conversational ball bouncing, but only Papa and Mr. Kennebrae hit it back.

Josie could think of nothing but Clarice's defection and feared if she spoke she'd inadvertently draw attention to her absent sister. Eli's silence unnerved her, and she kept glancing at him, hoping for some sign of how he was dealing with all this. The dessert dishes couldn't be cleared fast enough to suit Josie.

Just when she thought she might gracefully escape—was, in fact, just pushing back her chair—Mama's voice stopped her. "Josephine, please sit. We have some news for you."

Papa cleared his throat and looked stern.

Anxiety clawed its way up Josie's rib cage and danced in

her head. She looked from one face to the next, all staring at her, except Eli, who again contemplated the edge of the table.

Mr. Kennebrae, though somber, had a glitter in his eye that caused the hairs on Josie's arms to stand up. He couldn't contain a triumphant smile.

Papa cleared his throat again and rose, lifting his water glass. "Josephine..."

Uh-oh, this is serious. He remembered my name right off.

"We, your mother and I, have decided that, in light of Clarice disappointing us, you will take her place. The Kennebraes are amenable to this change. You will marry Eli."

Not a snatch of breathable air remained in the room. Josie blinked. That explained Mama's fake brightness and the mulish set to Grandma's jaw. It even explained Papa's determined look and Mr. Kennebrae's triumph. But what about Eli? She turned to him. He lifted his gaze to hers in a mute plea, though for what, she couldn't guess.

Indignation licked like fire through her. According to her father, any Zahn girl would do, and she was next in line. What about what she wanted? What about her promise to God to pursue her studies? What about being the woman God made her to be? Was all of it to be sucked away because she was needed to fill a quota in her father's schemes like another railcar of logs or unit of pine?

She straightened her back, hot words dancing on the tip of her tongue. They wouldn't coerce her like they had Clarice. And that was that.

Then Eli touched her hand, the merest whisper of a caress. She froze. He took a deep breath then gathered both her hands in his, turning in his chair to face her. "Josie, I'd hoped for some privacy to ask you, instead of having it announced like this."

She looked into his gentle eyes, drowning in his imploring gaze. What she saw there wasn't love, nor even affection, but a sort of calm desperation.

"But will you marry me?" His thumbs stroked the backs of her hands, warming the chilled shock from her fingers.

In spite of all she had meant to say, she found herself nodding, a wave of care for him crashing through her, extinguishing the fires of indignation to piles of steaming ash.

He kept hold of her hands in one of his while he reached into his pocket.

Papa and Mr. Kennebrae beamed. Papa raised his glass again. "This is wonderful. Abraham, later this week I'm hosting a picnic for all my workers as a thank-you for meeting a major contract deadline a month early. You and Eli should attend as my guests, and we'll announce the engagement then. If we get it all out in the open, hopefully things will all blow over then, and we can put this unpleasantness behind us."

Josie looked down at her left hand, noting the pale gray smudges where she hadn't been able to get all the ink off completely, trying to ignore the huge sparkling diamond Eli had put on her finger—the huge sparkling diamond she'd helped him pick out for Clarice. Evidently one Zahn girl was the same as another to Eli, too.

twelve

For two long days, Josie tried to settle her mind and escape into her work. She sketched and erased, figured and reworked until her head ached, trying not to think about the matter of her engagement. Her eyes burned from lack of sleep and poring over ship plans.

Giselle bounced into Josie's room and wrinkled her nose. "Mama wants you downstairs, Josie. She's got a visitor."

"Is it Mrs. Jefferson?" Josie knew Giselle didn't like the florid Mrs. Jefferson, who pinched little girls' cheeks and talked too loudly.

"No, it's a fat man. With a yellow vest and shiny shoes. He's sitting in Papa's chair, and he has whiskers like a badger."

Mystified, Josie stood up. She checked her reflection in the mirror, combed her hair, and straightened her dress, brushing the wrinkles from her skirt. She hoped his visit wouldn't take long. Work was the only thing that took her mind off her engagement.

Mr. Fox scooted to the edge of his chair and stood when she entered the parlor. He waited until she drew near and held out her hand, as she knew Mama expected her to do. "How do you do?" He took her fingers in his beefy grip, lingering over his greeting.

When he finally let go, she resisted the urge to wipe her hand on her dress.

"Josephine, this is Mr. Fox. He's the owner of Keystone Steel and Shipping."

Fox waited until she was seated before speaking. "We've met briefly before. Miss Zahn, I hear congratulations are in order." He grinned, ingratiatingly, over his tea cup. "I'm sure you've made a sound match."

Mama beamed. "We're all very happy with the way things have worked out."

"Thank you, Mr. Fox." Josie kept her tone neutral. Something about the way this man looked at her unsettled her. What was he doing here in the middle of the workday? If he had business with Papa, why didn't he go to the sawmill office?

He set his cup down, the chair creaking as he leaned forward. "I understand you received quite a ring from young Kennebrae."

Josie clenched her fist and put her right hand over her left. But Mama gushed and twittered. "Oh my, yes. A beautiful ring, and large enough to gratify a girl's heart that her betrothed won't be stingy with her in the future. Do show it to him, Josephine."

She had no choice but to hold her hand out. Mama scowled at her, and she realized she was glaring at Fox. Schooling her features, she tried to appear the blushing bride. The entire charade irked her.

"Stunning. You're to be commended, Miss Zahn. When is the happy event?" Fox slid predatory eyes toward her hand. No doubt he saw everything in terms of acquisition and victory.

"We haven't set a date yet." Josie accepted a cup of tea from her mother but didn't drink. Her stomach roiled, something in her recoiling from Fox's calculating, insinuating gaze.

He leaned forward to pick up his cup from the low table before him. The china rattled, and he jumped back. "Oh, how careless of me." The cup rocked on its side in the saucer, tea covering the table and dripping to the floor. His pant leg had received a liberal splattering as well, and his fingers dripped. "I'm so sorry, Mrs. Zahn. Do you perhaps have a washroom where I could clean up?"

Mama, who had bounced out of her chair at the first clink of china, rang for the maid. "Show Mr. Fox to the facilities, please. And don't worry, Gervase, no harm done. I'll get another cup for you."

The moment the washroom door at the top of the stairs closed, Josie frowned at her mother. "Mama, I don't like that man. Did you have to talk to him about the engagement? About the ring?"

"Josephine Elizabeth Zahn"—Mama jerked her hand away and used the tray cloth to mop up the spilled tea—"don't take that tone with me. He's a respected businessman in this city, and he came to wish you well in your marriage. He moves in high circles in this town, and you will not antagonize him." Mama glared at Josie over her shoulder. "You'll be cordial to him and show some grace. I didn't spend every day of the last many years drilling manners into your head to have you embarrass me this way."

Josie bit her tongue and took the tray into the kitchen for the cook to reset.

Fox was gone a long time, and when he reappeared at the foot of the stairs, he slid his watch into his hand and refused Mama's offers of more tea and cakes. "It's been delightful, Mrs. Zahn, but I'm afraid I must fly. Businesses, as you well know, don't run themselves." He clasped Josie's limp hand and crushed her fingers in a hearty grip. "And, Miss Zahn, I wish you every happiness in your upcoming marriage." He bared his yellow teeth, flipped his hat onto his bushy gray hair, and departed, the door slamming briskly behind his rotund figure.

Josie breathed out a sigh of relief at his leaving and this time wiped her hand on her skirt. Obnoxious little man. He looked as if he were trying to figure out how to beat her at some game she didn't even know she was playing.

She returned to her room and sank onto her desk chair. "Giselle? Antoinette? Where are you little hoydens?" Her papers and books were strewn across the desk, as if someone had accidentally swept them to the floor and hastily piled them back up. She rose and headed to the nursery the little girls still shared. When were they going to learn to keep out of her things?

⁂

Josie crossed her arms at her waist and leaned against the slender bole of a young maple tree. Children ran and women laughed. Men played horseshoes and talked, and wafting over the noise of happy picnickers was the smell of roasting chickens and mustard-laden potato salad. Flags and bunting flapped in the breeze, festooning the pavilion in gay colors. Brawny lumbermen cavorted like kids, nodding with broad smiles each time one of them passed her.

"Your father will be looking for you soon." Grandma Bess hitched her black bag higher on her arm. "The Kennebraes should be here in a little while."

"Are you sure he's looking for me? Or will any of his daughters do?" Josie rubbed the underside of her engagement ring with her thumb, twisting the big diamond in the sunlight.

"What kind of question is that?"

"I don't understand him. I don't understand so much right now." The need to talk to someone made the words pour from her throat. "How can he be so unfeeling to his own family and yet so generous to his workers? Half the time he doesn't even remember my name, but he'll throw a party that has his workers falling all over themselves to tell me what a wonderful boss he is."

Grandma tugged her arm and led her to a nearby park bench. "Your father can be as thick as two planks sometimes. I know. This picnic was my idea, actually. It would never occur to your father to do something like this."

"How did you talk him into it then?"

"I told him happy workers were productive workers."

"So you showed him how he would benefit from it, and he agreed to do something nice. That's just like him. Never do something for nothing." Josie tightened her lips in disapproval.

"You're too harsh on him. He isn't unkind, just a bit thoughtless. He needs a nudge in the right direction from time to time, that's all." Grandma dug in her bag for a magazine.

"Are all men like Papa?" Josie twisted her ring again, still unaccustomed to the weight of it on her hand. "Are they all just a bit thoughtless?"

"By 'all men' I assume you mean Eli?" Grandma folded the cover of the magazine back and scanned the table of contents.

Josie didn't answer, not sure what to say. Though she'd imagined herself engaged to Eli Kennebrae a thousand times in her girlish dreams, the reality had turned out much different. This ring was just the most prominent example of how wrong things were. She was everyone's second best.

"I think"—Grandma flipped another page—"that you should talk to Eli. You should get to know him and let him get to know you. You might both be surprised by what you find. And, Josie, you don't have to stand by and take this, not from your parents, not from Eli. If you're truly unsuited to wed, you should say so. But not before you give it a chance. From what I can tell, Eli Kennebrae is a bright, caring, good man. He's still a man, though, which means he's not a mind reader. If you want something from him, or you want him to know something, you're going to have to tell him."

"How do I tell him I want to pursue my studies in higher mathematics? How do I tell him that I despise this ring and everything it stands for? How do I tell him that just when I was sure I had things mapped out, that I had figured out just what God wanted me to do, my whole world got thrown into an uproar, with Eli Kennebrae right in the middle of it?"

Grandma chuckled, licked her finger, and turned a glossy page. "You have plenty of questions, that's plain. Have you prayed about any of them? How do you know what Eli's reaction to your gift for numbers will be if you never reveal that gift to him? Is it fair to harbor a grudge about that ring when Eli has no idea how you feel about it? And have you considered that marrying Eli might be what God had in store for you all along?"

Before Josie could answer, girlish squeals erupted in the pavilion. She rose, her mouth falling open.

Eli was wheeling Mr. Kennebrae's chair toward the pavilion, and at the same moment, Clarice and Geoffrey returned, hand in hand.

"Now might be a good time for you to go up there. Your mama might need you to spread a little oil on the water." Grandma stood and used her magazine as a sunshade. "The little girls look happy to see Clarice."

"Aren't you coming?" Josie didn't want to go up the slope alone.

"Plenty of drama up there without my adding to it. I'll wait here." She settled herself on the bench again and resumed reading.

When Josie reached the pavilion, the atmosphere of tension clogged her lungs like soot. Clarice lifted wide, imploring eyes to her. Papa's face resembled a November gale, cold and forbidding, while Mama sat in a wicker chair fanning herself, darting worried glances between her husband and her daughter with the occasional nasty look for her brand-new son-in-law.

Geoffrey stood behind Clarice with his hand protectively on her shoulder. His jaw muscles stood out and his legs were braced, as if to do battle.

Abraham Kennebrae's eyes drilled each person he looked at. Red flushed his hollow cheeks, and the breeze ruffled his white hair.

Beside him, Eli blew out a long breath. His eyes found Josie's.

The lid would blow off this tea kettle in a moment. Josie found herself moving forward, her mouth stretching in a smile she didn't feel. "Clarice, Geoffrey, welcome home." She embraced her sister's stiff shoulders and whispered, "Cheer up. It will all blow over." Josie turned to Geoffrey. "I've always wanted a brother. Welcome to the family, Geoffrey. I know Clarice will be very happy with you." She stood on tiptoe and kissed his rock-hard cheek. Josie walked over to Eli and slid her arm through his. "Things have worked out so well, Clarice. You got Geoffrey, and I got Eli." She gazed up into Eli's stunned eyes, begging him to catch on, to back her up.

Eli caught her meaning, for he stepped forward and held out his hand to Geoffrey. "Congratulations, Geoff." He smiled, shook his friend's hand, and cuffed him on the shoulder. "She's a great girl." He winked, then leaned down and kissed Clarice's rosy cheek. "I'd say my loss is your gain, but I don't think anybody lost here."

Josie could almost see the gears turning over in Mama's mind. Mama sat upright and stopped waving her handkerchief under her chin. All around them, the workers crowded, eyes watching, ears alert. Papa cleared his throat, unclenching his hands. Mama nudged him in the side.

Papa donned his making-the-best-of-things face. "As you can see, things have worked out for the best. Clarice, Geoffrey, welcome home." He motioned for the servers to begin dishing up the food for the gathered workers.

Though conscious of the uneasiness remaining, Josie blew out a breath she didn't realize she'd been holding.

Clarice clasped Josie's hand and lifted it to examine the

diamond ring. "You're marrying Eli?" The words were hissed into Josie's ear.

She nodded. "Papa and Mr. Kennebrae still wanted the wedding, so Papa figured I'd do just as well."

"But what about your studies? I thought you were going to college."

The muddle of Josie's thoughts and feelings sloshed about in her chest. "I don't know what I'm going to do. I thought I had everything figured out, but now. . ." The little girls swarmed around Clarice, and Josie found herself once more beside Eli.

Abraham Kennebrae wrapped her wrist in one of his bony hands and gave her a squeeze. "You're a good girl, Josephine Zahn. I saw how you handled that situation. You'll make an excellent Kennebrae. You've got smarts and tact, just like my Genevieve had." The hand around her wrist tightened painfully. "What's *he* doing here?"

Josie followed his glare. Her scalp crinkled. Duluth wasn't such a small place that she should keep running into Gervase Fox.

Fox's eyes swept the assembly, stopping when they landed on the Kennebraes. He lost no time weaving his way through the picnic tables. "Abraham, Eli, and Miss Zahn, you look even more fetching than you did yesterday." He bowed to Josie.

Eli wrapped his arm around Josie's waist and tucked her firmly into his side. "You've met?" His whisper brushed her temple, taking her breath away.

"He called on my mother yesterday." The warmth of Eli's embrace surrounded her. His side was rock hard, as was his arm around her. If she didn't know better, she'd think he was trying to protect her from something.

"Another successful Kennebrae wedding." Mr. Fox bowed and grinned at her. "Though this one might not sew up the shipping contracts quite as neatly as the previous two."

Abraham sucked in a breath. "What do you mean, Fox?"

"Just that I've been talking with Radcliffe Zahn. He sees no reason why he should tie himself down to exclusive contracts, not if someone else can do the job more efficiently."

"You bounder. How dare you come in here and try to steal business from me!" Mr. Kennebrae pounded his chair arm.

"Steal? It's not stealing. It's business. Zahn feels that the best shipper should haul his goods. If you have the best ship, you get the contract."

"We'll see about that." Abraham jerked his head at Eli. "Take me to Radcliffe."

Eli stood still a long moment, his arm remaining firmly around Josie.

Geoffrey, as if sensing the need for his presence, slipped alongside. "We'll all go, Mr. Kennebrae. I'm anxious to hear what Zahn has to say." He grasped the steering bar on the back of the chair.

Eli drew Josie with him as he fell into step with his lawyer.

❧

Eli's gut churned. Fox couldn't be trusted. He was wily and persuasive. Grandfather's plans looked to be going up in the smoke of Fox's schemes.

Zahn, when they drew near, shifted in his seat and poked his now-congealed potato salad with his fork.

"Zahn, what's this Fox is spewing? Are you going back on our agreement?"

Eli grimaced at Grandfather's direct approach. All the delicacy of a steam-powered ice breaker.

"Agreement? I'm not going back on anything, but business is business. Gervase tells me he can haul my lumber faster and in greater quantities than anyone on the lakes." Zahn put his fork down. "I can't pass up something like that, not if it's true."

Eli shot a glance at Fox, who rocked on his heels, a smug smile plastered on his face. He looked like a bear sucking on a fistful of honey. Josie's hand on Eli's arm gripped tight.

Grandfather looked ready to explode, his face growing red, his long, bony fingers gripping the arms of his chair hard enough to leave dents in the walnut.

Eli shook his head. "He's hornswoggled you, Mr. Zahn. Nothing on the lake will beat the *Bethany* when she's done. Not for speed, capacity, or loading time."

"Don't be so sure." Fox leered. "You're not the only one with new ideas in lumber shipping." Gervase leaned over the table and plucked an apple from the fruit bowl in the center. He polished it against his lapel then sank his teeth into it like a wolf on a rabbit's neck. "Why don't you put your ship to the test? That would settle things nicely."

Eli shook his head, refusing any kind of a wager, sensing a trap.

But Grandfather wasn't so cautious. "You're on. A race between your ship and the *Bethany*, winner gets the Zahn contract." He waggled his bushy eyebrows at Zahn, who looked bemused and interested. "Say, the first weekend in November? First ship to get to Two Harbors, load up, and return to Duluth wins the contract?"

The first weekend in November? They'd never be ready by then. Eli grabbed Grandfather's shoulder, but the old man shook him off.

"That all right with you, Zahn?" Fox checked, an eager gleam lighting his cold gray eyes.

Radcliffe nodded. "That sounds fair."

"Then we're agreed. But don't be sorry when you don't win. My ship's the fastest on the lake." Fox dug in his coat pocket for a fat cigar. He seemed to remember the ladies present, for he merely stuck it between his fingers and punctuated the air with it instead of lighting it.

Grandfather reacted as if he'd been stung. "I'm so sure the *Bethany* will win, that if she doesn't, you can have her."

Eli blinked, fear clawing up his spine. *No.* "Grandfather!" He swallowed, shocked at the old man's rash declaration. "You can't promise that."

"I can promise anything I want to. I'm still head of this family and head of Kennebrae Shipping."

Fox stuffed the cigar between his moist lips, a nasty smile climbing his face. "That'll do just fine, Abraham. I know your word is good. After all, how many times have you told me that once a Kennebrae makes a promise, he keeps it, no matter what?" He turned on his heel and left the shelter.

Unbearable pressure tightened around Eli's lungs and brain. A little less than a month to have all the conversions made to the *Bethany* and have her seaworthy enough to beat Gervase Fox's fastest ship.

Josie slipped her hand into his, her eyes watching the departing figure. She seemed to sense the enormity of what had just happened. If the *Bethany* lost, the pride of the Kennebrae fleet would go to Fox. Fox would win what he couldn't buy. Grandfather had fallen neatly into his trap.

The afternoon passed, though Eli was barely conscious of anything beyond his own scrambled thoughts. The ride home to Kennebrae House seemed hours long. Eli blew out a long breath.

Grandfather alternately fumed and fretted over the way Fox had suckered him into the race.

"Well, can we do it?" Grandfather poked Eli in the side.

"Now's a fine time to be asking me that."

"Stop being facetious and answer my question." His black eyes burned hot with a demand that Eli come through for him with the answer he wanted to hear.

"I hope so. I'll try."

"You'll try? Don't you understand the pressure we're

under?" As usual, Grandfather's worry came out in a verbal assault against those around him. Eli was fed up to the back teeth.

"Understand? You're the one who doesn't understand. You walked right into this buzz saw. And you're dragging me with you. I'm the only one who really understands what you've done. And gambling! You know better. Kennebraes have never wagered before, especially not for something so stupid as a lumber contract. We may very well lose this ship and our reputation, and why? Because you couldn't resist rising to Fox's bait. He laid his trap, and *wham*! You jumped right into it."

The carriage driver slowed and looked back over his shoulder.

Eli realized he was shouting. Shame licked his cheeks. He struggled with himself and modulated his voice. "I'm doing the best I can, and so are the men. The ship will be ready. How she'll fare against Fox's ship is anybody's guess."

"That's not good enough. We have to win."

Eli took a healthy grip on his temper. He could do nothing at the moment. But as soon as he got home, he'd get to work on a new schedule. Grandfather would have to turn loose more cash to pay the workers overtime.

thirteen

Josie sat up and punched her pillow into a tighter wad. Her nightgown tangled about her knees, and she trod back the covers. The faint familiar blast of a steamship whistle traveled over the water from the harbor. Rolling to her side, she stared at the pale square of moonlight streaming through the window and tracking slowly across the floor.

From the stairwell, the clock chimed twice. "Lord, why can't I make my mind slow down? Seems the harder I try to get to sleep, the more awake I become."

Grandma Bess had told Josie once that being unable to sleep was a great opportunity to flex one's prayer muscles and talk to God. "God never sleeps, and quite often if I'm wide awake at night, He's got something He wants to say to me, or there's something He's waiting to hear me say."

Josie sat up, wrapped her arms around her updrawn legs, and put her chin on her knees. Her braid fell over her shoulder. "I'm in a muddle, Lord, though I guess You know that better than anyone." Her engagement ring glittered in the faint starshine. "All my feelings are in a muddle, too. I don't know what I want. I don't know what *You* want. I thought I wanted to marry Eli, but then he was engaged to Clarice. I tried so hard to kill my feelings for him, to focus on my mathematics. I thought You wanted me to pursue my studies and forget about Eli Kennebrae."

She sighed and slid out of bed to walk to the window. Drawing the curtain aside, she studied the gaudy diamond on her left hand. "This ring screams out everything that's wrong with my engagement. I'm Eli's second best. The next one in line. Any Zahn girl would do as far as my father is concerned. Am I wrong to want more? To want Eli to love me for myself? To love me the way I know I could love him?"

A shaft of honesty drove through her mind. *Could* love Eli? She *did* love Eli. With everything in her. She knew it as surely as she knew her own name. She stood at the window for a long time. Finally, after coming to terms with her feelings for Eli, peace filled her. She would go through with the marriage, and she would have enough love for both of them. Half a loaf was better than none, wasn't it? And by marrying him, she would honor her parents.

She twisted the ring on her finger. And she would stop despising this hunk of jewelry. It wasn't her choice, but instead of thinking of how much she disliked it, she would think of the giver instead.

Refreshed in mind, she decided to peruse the hatch cover drawings once more before trying to sleep. The original design had bothered her from the start. There had to be a better, more secure way to fasten the hatches.

She lit her lamp and drew the blueprints from the bedside table. Careful not to step on the spot beside her desk that creaked, she dug in a bottom drawer and pulled out the parcel that had arrived for her from her tutor just that day. Those hatches had plagued her since she first saw Eli's original design, and feeling uncertain of her abilities in this area, she'd written to Mr. Clement for his guidance. How she missed her bald-headed, bespectacled tutor and friend. If anyone could help her with the ship design, he could.

She opened the package and took out two books and a note. Josie settled into bed and unfolded the paper, a wave of affection and loneliness sweeping over her as she read his familiar, perfect handwriting.

My dear Josie,
I'm very pleased you've found a way to apply all that

knowledge you worked so hard to gain under my tutelage.
None of my students here in Detroit matches you for intellect,
and I find myself bored with them.

Here are two books I thought might help you with the
questions you posed regarding the hatch design. Maybe you
should back up and consider it from another angle. If you still
need help with it, I can pose the problem to the shipbuilders here,
but you led me to believe the work was highly confidential.

Which reminds me, I had an inquiry last week about you
and the work you might be doing in Duluth. He refused
to tell me for whom he worked, which made me suspicious.
He seemed more interested in confirming that you were my
student and that your abilities were more reliable than just
what you are working on at the moment. I sent the fellow
away with a flea in his ear. But if someone knows enough
to be asking me about you, I'd be careful. The shipbuilding
industry can be quite cutthroat.

Sincerely,
K. Clement

Cutthroat. With the race looming ahead of her, with Eli's
reputation as a shipbuilder on the line, as well as the fate of
the *Bethany*, cutthroat just about described things. And who
would ask after her from her former tutor? Should she tell
Geoffrey about it? Or was it Geoffrey himself, checking up
on her work?

She thrust those thoughts to the back of her mind and
forced herself to concentrate. She paged through one of the
books Mr. Clement had sent, scratched notes on a tablet,
and chewed the end of her pencil. How could she improve
this design to not only make it watertight—a must—but
also ensure it would work with the cranes on the loading
dock? Eli's initial design would make it simple to remove
the hatches to keep them out of the way for loading, but the

hinges he'd designed for easy use wouldn't hold against the strain of a severe storm. . .or even a moderate one.

She set the first book aside and picked up the second. Railroad design? A paper marker jutted from the middle of the book, and she opened to that page. A diagram of the rod and pin design for coupling railroad cars. Similar to Eli's design. She frowned. Why had Clement sent a book on railroads? She checked his note once more.

Maybe you should back up and consider it from another angle.

She flipped to the next page. Like a photographer's flash the answer to the problem of how to safely seal the hatches scorched her mind. That was it! A knuckle coupler.

Josie scribbled out a few notes, double-checked her calculations, and flopped back against the pillows. That was it. The idea would take a little polishing, but how simple. She'd have to write to Mr. Clement in the morning.

Pride of accomplishment and happy anticipation of what Eli would say drew her from the bed. She twirled on the patterned rug, her nightgown flaring out, catching the moonlight. Her braid whipped around as she danced a jig.

Then her face fell, her feet became still. She wouldn't get to hear what Eli would say when he was presented with the solution to the last major obstacle to construction. Geoffrey would. Geoffrey would take her papers and ideas and present them to Eli as coming from Professor Josephson.

Yet another barrier to her happiness. When she'd conceived the professor, she never imagined she would marry Eli. Now the secret stood between them like a seawall. Her decision to marry Eli would mean forever keeping the professor's identity a secret. Forever hiding from her husband her mathematical abilities.

With her feelings more jumbled than ever, she slid under the covers. She'd have to get word to Geoffrey as soon as possible.

❧

Eli strode along the deep-carpeted hallway of the top floor of Kennebrae Shipping. He carried a folder of drawings and figures, tapping his thigh as he walked. The correspondence from Professor Josephson had started the day off right.

A smile tugged at Eli's lips, and his mind raced with all the things he needed to get done now that the final drawings were in his hand. The solution had turned out to be so simple he didn't know why he hadn't seen it himself. The oppression and desperation that weighed him down ever since Grandfather had argued with Fox at the picnic lifted like lake fog in a stiff breeze.

He just needed to get through one more meeting with Grandfather, one more look at the budget for the modifications, one more discussion of plans and workforce and security. And for the first time in weeks, he didn't dread the meeting. His goal was within reach. He would be able to look Grandfather in the eye, present him with the finished *Bethany*, and take his place with his brothers as an asset to Kennebrae Shipping. He would be needed and appreciated and a true Kennebrae.

The conference room sat empty. Grandfather must be running late.

Eli started toward his customary seat then stopped himself. No, this time he would sit where he could see the painting, look the titan in the eyes and smile. Maybe his own painting would hang somewhere in this room someday. And now that he had accomplished his goal, or nearly so, he felt he had earned his place.

He spread his papers out on the table, organizing them into categories for discussion—financing, supplies, workers, timetables. If things went well, they could be through the particulars and Eli could be back down at the shipyard before lunch.

The door opened and Grandfather wheeled in.

Eli took in the paper-white skin, the slight tremble of the left hand. Concern gripped his heart. . .and dread. How much longer would Grandfather be with them?

"Tell me you've made some progress." The old man's voice pierced the silence, as strong and commanding as ever.

"Professor Josephson came through with the final plans for the hatch covers, and we should be able to manufacture and install them in less than two weeks." Eli slid the drawings across the table.

"Two weeks? The race is in two weeks!" Grandfather snatched up the papers. He scanned the pages, shuffling through them quickly. "You'll have to move quicker than that. And have you met this professor yet? Are you sure you can trust him? Don't underestimate Fox. He's sneaky. He'd stoop to anything to win this race."

Eli bit back a sigh and forced his voice to sound cheerful. "No, Grandfather, I haven't met the professor, and yes, I trust him. He hasn't steered us wrong yet. And you may not like Fox, but be careful what you say about him. You don't want a nasty slander lawsuit on your hands."

"Don't tell me what to do. Find out who this professor is. For all we know, he's a spy for Fox. We can't be too careful. He'll do anything to win."

Eli refrained from telling Grandfather to stop telling *him* what to do. "Josephson doesn't want any contact. He's a recluse, I told you that. I thought you'd be happy with the progress, not picking and poking and looking for something to complain about."

Grandfather perused the rest of the papers, marking his initials against the spending chits.

Eli breathed a sigh of relief when the papers were returned

to the folder. He pushed back his chair and glanced up at the portrait, giving the painting a wink.

"Don't leave just yet." Grandfather motioned him back to his seat. "I want your assurance you'll track down this professor character and have him thoroughly checked out. Something about this situation isn't ringing true. I have a bad feeling."

Eli stared at the folder before him. "I'm not saying the situation isn't a bit odd, but who am I to look a gift horse in the mouth? Josephson is saving my bacon with these drawings and calculations. Without his help, I never would've made it this far. And don't forget, if you hadn't been drawn into this ridiculous race, I wouldn't be under such pressure to finish the ship in two weeks."

"I know it." Grandfather shoved his chair back from the table and lifted his shaky hand to smooth his hair. "My temper and my tongue get the better of me from time to time. I should know better, but there it is. I jumped in, and I'll move heaven and earth to win now."

Eli shook his head. "Fox knew just how to provoke you. But with these final plans, we're almost home free." He itched to leave, to get started on the last modifications.

"You'll think I'm a silly old man, getting us into this trouble. But I've never held back, never been afraid to leap first and figure out the details later. And when I give my word, I keep it. I guess that's why Zahn's behavior galls me so. I know we never signed a formal contract with the marriage, but he led me to believe a union between our families would cement a union between our companies. I was more angry at his waffling in front of Fox than I was about Fox's outrageous statements and horning in at the picnic. I thought I knew Zahn's character better. I'm beginning to think forcing you into marriage with one of his girls might've been a mistake."

Eli gripped the arms of the chair, the brass studs marching

down the leather making indentions in his fingers. "What about your promise to Grandmother? Your heart condition?" His mouth went dry.

Grandfather shrugged and stared at the fireplace at the end of the room, not meeting Eli's eyes. "Well, maybe I put it stronger than necessary. Your grandmother wanted you married to good girls, that's true."

Eli's arms trembled. "And what about your heart condition?"

That infuriating shrug again. "I saw a specialist, and he said it might not be quite as serious as I led you to believe."

Eli shot out of his chair, knocking his folder of papers across the glossy surface in a fan of pages. "You mean to tell me you lied about dying?"

"Not lied. . .exactly." Grandfather made tamping down motions with his hands. "Just maybe exaggerated the seriousness of the situation. I knew nothing else would budge you. You looked like a man holding a governor's pardon when you found out Clarice had eloped. I didn't intend to give up so easy."

"Exaggerated." Eli leaned close, bracing his hands on the table. "Do you or do you not have a heart ailment?"

Grandfather glared at Eli. "That's not important. What's important is your winning this race."

Eli ground his teeth. "And did you or did you not promise Grandmother that you would find us all brides before you died?"

"I surely did. And I aim to see that promise through, if I have to drag you to the altar." He glared at Eli. "Enough of this talk. I want you to find this professor, fix the hatches on the *Bethany*, and win that race." Abraham Kennebrae, stubborn and unrepentant, never backed down. Eli tapped together his papers and left before he did or said something he'd regret.

fourteen

Eli twirled his walking stick and glanced up at a sky so blue it hurt the eyes. A ton weight had fallen from his shoulders like an enormous, land-bound ship sliding off the ways and splashing into the lake with the last of Josephson's calculations. The hatch idea was brilliant.

And he had to admit a bit of relief since finding out the previous day that his grandfather wasn't in imminent danger of dying. Heart ailment. The old man would outlive them all on sheer force of will.

The pressure to finish the job still surrounded him and the race loomed large before him, but in spite of those things, he found himself whistling as he sauntered up the Zahns' walkway. At last he felt he had time to give in to the thoughts that had plagued him for many days.

Thoughts of Josie Zahn.

He couldn't even say why he was here, for he had more than enough things to keep him busy at the shipyard, but after fighting the urge all morning, he finally gave in. He had to see her.

He twisted the bell on the center of the door, listening to the buzzing ring muffled on the other side. Perhaps he should've brought flowers. Or candy. Girls liked those kinds of things. He shrugged. Next time.

The curtain in the window darkened, and the door flew open. Giselle stared up at him for a moment, then her face split in a smile to match his own. "Oh, Mr. Kennebrae, have you come to take us on another outing?" She stepped back and held the door wide.

"Sorry, not today, sweetheart. Today I've come to see Josie. Is she in?" He stepped inside and removed his hat.

Antoinette bounced down the stairs and stopped at the landing.

Grandma Bess looked up from her chair in the parlor, letting her magazine drop into her lap.

Antoinette grabbed the rounded balustrade and shouted upstairs over her shoulder. "Josie, somebody to see you!"

Giselle giggled and took Eli's hand, swinging it while grinning at him. "It's your beau!"

Eli chuckled and didn't know where to look. Little-girl eyes were everywhere.

"Giselle, enough of your nonsense." Grandma Bess levered herself up with her cane. "Take his things and get back to your needlework. Your mother will expect to see some progress on that sampler before she gets home." She swatted the little girl's behind as Giselle scooted past her. "Good afternoon, Mr. Kennebrae. Very nice to see you again. Won't you come in and sit down? No doubt Josie heard someone's"—she sent a pointed glance up to Antoinette—"unladylike bellowing informing her of your arrival. She'll be down directly."

Eli, now without his hat or walking stick, didn't know what to do with his hands. He hoped Josie wouldn't be long.

Giselle stared at him over the top of a square of cloth, poking a needle in and out in a pattern he couldn't discern.

He sat opposite her, on a camelback sofa, uncomfortable in this decidedly feminine room. Ferns hung from the ceiling and flowed out of white urns. Bric-a-brac covered every surface—pictures in frames, shells, figurines. Oils and watercolors covered the walls. Overhead a chandelier, unlit at midday, hung from a plaster medallion of whorls, loops, and vines.

"I'm sorry Octavia isn't here to greet you. She's gone over to Clarice's new home to help her settle in. Things here have been in a complete uproar since the elopement." The old woman didn't seem to care that she was crashing about on a topic people had been studiously avoiding bringing up to Eli. "How are things at the shipyard?" Grandma Bess picked up her magazine. "Your grandfather sure landed you in the soup, didn't he? Old men can be so silly sometimes. Everything's a competition. Anyone could see Gervase Fox was baiting Abraham, and like a tethered bear, Abraham snarled back. And you're the one who has to pay for it." She turned a page. "Abraham always was half genius, half foolish."

Eli, taken aback at her forthright speech, cast about for something to say that wouldn't be disloyal to Grandfather.

She smiled at him, her eyes nearly buried in wrinkles. "I can tell I've surprised you, saying what I think. But I'm an old woman, and I've earned the right. I don't have time for shilly-shallying, and most people, when they get over the shock, find it refreshing. I've known your grandfather for twenty-five years or more. Knew your grandmother, too. Genevieve and I were great friends once upon a time. Salt of the earth, that woman, and loved your grandfather something fierce. I always felt a bit sorry for her, though, loving him like she did, and him so busy with his empire. He never seemed to get around to loving her back."

Eli frowned. "You don't think he loved her?"

"I think he did, in his own way, and it was only after she passed on that he realized how much he'd lost. He spent his time traveling and putting business before family. And he missed all he could've shared with Genevieve if he would've stayed home and cherished her for the treasure she was." She slapped the magazine closed and stuffed it into a black bag at her feet. "You'd be wise to learn from his example, Eli. No woman wants to come second in her husband's affection, be it to another woman, a business, or just his own pride and ambition."

"I think I understand what you mean." He laced his fingers

together, leaning forward and putting his elbows on his knees.

"I hope you do. This marriage business isn't one to be taken lightly, and it isn't something that should be decided for you by someone else. My son and your grandfather think that anyone, provided he or she is of similar faith and social status, should be able to have an amiable marriage. But people aren't that tidy. You take Josie now. Josie's a girl in a thousand, and if you take the time to get to know her, you'll find she's of the caliber of your grandmother. Steel true, blade straight. And brighter than anyone around here gives her credit for. But that won't do you any good if you only take her at face value. Take the time to dig deeper, find out what kind of girl she really is."

The way she looked at Eli, sizing him up like he was a nailhead and she was holding a hammer, made him want to squirm. Josie chose that minute to enter, and he bolted out of his seat. "Hello."

She had her hair coiled up on the back of her head in a thick, shiny braid. He wondered what it would look like all loose and flowing around her shoulders. The thought made him swallow hard. Only a husband would be privileged to see a woman with her hair down. When she stepped near, the smell of violets surrounded him, taking him back to his childhood. Grandmother had grown African violets by the dozens in her conservatory—tiny pink, purple, and white blossoms that appeared to float above velvet green heart-shaped leaves.

"Hello." She watched him, a reserved expression on her face but pleasant enough.

For a long moment he studied her then realized he was staring like an idiot. "Hello."

A smile teased her lips. "You already said that."

What was the matter with him? He'd never had trouble

talking to her before. "I, uh, I came to see you." He felt Giselle's and Grandma Bess's eyes staring at him, but none affected him like Josie's, deep blue, nearly purple.

Grandma Bess snorted. "Why don't you two go out to the garden? It's more private there."

Eli shot her a grateful glance and offered his arm to Josie.

She took it, tilting her head to look up at him. "Would you like to see Mama's roses?"

The lake breeze cleared his head a bit. They walked down the flagstone path between rioting beds of flowers. Lilac bushes, long bereft of flowers, outlined the boundaries of the garden. Arches of climbing roses spanned the paths, nodding in the sunshine, sending showers of petals like pink snow to the grass.

"They're Mama's pride and joy. She tends them so carefully. Each fall she prunes them and covers them with straw and weighs them down with newspaper and stones. The climate is so harsh here, but she manages to keep them alive and thriving."

He didn't care about roses or gardening, but he found himself enjoying listening to her talk. She led him to a bench that overlooked the lake. The slap and scrape of the waves against the rocky shore provided a familiar background noise.

She settled in, smoothing her skirts and crossing her ankles in a purely feminine way. Her hands were so small, the diamond on her finger hung like an enormous drop of dew. Something about that ring disquieted him. Though he enjoyed the idea of being engaged to her, that ring didn't look quite right.

He did have something that she'd like better. But how to give it to her? The opal ring in its velvet box burned a hole in his pocket. His heart swelled a bit at the thought of having just the right gift, something he knew would make her happy. He gave himself a mental pat on the back for stopping off at the jeweler's on the way over to pick it up for her.

"How are things coming at the shipyard?"

He tore his gaze away from her hands. "Good now. I've solved the last major hurdle. Well, not me, exactly. Another engineer I've been working with. He came up with an absolutely ingenious design for the loading hatches. That problem has stumped us for weeks now."

She moistened her lips and looked up at the house on the slight slope above them. "And you'll be ready for the race?"

"Yes, and I just got word that Noah and Annie will be returning from their honeymoon soon. I can't tell you how relieved I am that Noah will be at the wheel of the *Bethany* for the race. Though he doesn't know about it all yet." Eli hoped Grandfather would be the one to break the news to Noah that the fate of his beloved ship was on the line. Noah, easygoing and gentle until pushed too far, just might blow his boiler when he found out how rash Grandfather had been. "I didn't come to talk about my ship, though, or the race."

"You didn't?"

"No, I'd like to talk about more pleasant things." He ventured to take her hand, thrilling when her fingers curled around his. "I think there are things about you that I don't know, but I'd very much like to. Things have been so snarled up between us, so cluttered with other people's wants and wishes, we've barely had time to get to know each other."

She chewed her lower lip lightly, her lashes hiding her eyes.

How could he break down this reserve of hers? When he had taken her to the circus, she had seemed so open and friendly, but ever since their engagement, it was as if a wall had grown up between them. "I suppose it isn't fair to ask you to reveal your secrets without being willing to share my own. I'll tell you one."

He ignored a thrust of vulnerability. "Ever since I was a little boy, I've dreamed of doing something big, something so important that my grandfather and my brothers would be amazed. I've always felt like the least important Kennebrae. Grandfather has an iron will and a Midas touch. Jonathan is a whiz at business and handling people. Noah is one of the youngest captains on the Great Lakes. . .and one of the best. And what have I done? Nothing. . .yet. The success of the *Bethany* means more than just winning this race. It means I'll have made my mark on the family business and on cargo shipping forever. I will have contributed to Kennebrae Shipping in a way that no other Kennebrae could have."

"Have your brothers made you feel unimportant? Has your grandfather said he feels you don't contribute?" Her delicate black brows arched.

"Not in so many words. It's just something I feel. Something I have to do for my own sake as much as the business's." He'd laid bare a part of his heart he'd hardly even acknowledged existed. He needed something in return from her to make it seem worthwhile. "What about you? Surely you have some dream or desire, something you've always wanted." As much as he needed her answer, he needed something to distract him from the thought running through his head continually since she walked into the parlor.

What would it be like to kiss her?

❧

Josie blinked. Did a dream you'd laid aside count?

The warmth of his palm pressing against hers distracted her. His hand tightened on hers. "You're hesitating. I'm sorry. I've pried too much. It was forward of me to ask you to reveal a secret." He looked so forlorn and alone, her heart wanted to cry.

"No, it isn't that." She returned the pressure of his grip. "It's just that it's hard to put into words the things I want."

His eyes glowed and a smile brightened his expression. "I suppose you want what most women want. A home, a family."

It pained her how little he really knew her. Not that she didn't want a home and a family, but what about everything else she wanted? She had a calling, something she was compelled to do.

She studied their locked hands. Josie Kennebrae. Mrs. Eli Kennebrae. Heat shot up her cheeks, and her breath caught in her throat. Part of her thrilled at the idea, and part of her quailed.

When she married him, she would be obeying her parents, but would she also be disobeying God? She'd promised God she would be the woman He made her to be, that she would use her gifts for His glory. How could she do that if she married? No husband would allow his wife to be an engineer. "Would you like to know what I really want?"

"Tell me." He pressed her fingers, making the cold diamond band bite into her finger, reminding her of who he had bought it for.

"I want to be treated like an individual instead of one of many. I'm tired of being known as one of the Zahn girls. When people look at me, I want them to see me. I want. . ."

"When you marry me, you won't be a Zahn girl anymore. You'll be a Kennebrae." His voice sounded deep and rumbly, and his eyes bored into hers.

She jerked when his hand came up and touched her cheek. She swallowed, her mouth dry.

"Josie?" He leaned close. His eyes asked permission just before his lips came down on hers.

It was more wondrous and breathtaking than she'd even imagined. His arms came around her and drew her to him. The warmth of his lips seared through her. Her hand came up and touched the faint roughness of his cheek. Love for him coursed over her. If only she could stay here in his arms forever, loving and beloved.

Cold reality dashed over her, freezing her like an icy wave.

She might love him, but he didn't love her. He didn't even know her. She was just the next Zahn girl in line. Her hands came up and thrust against his chest, breaking the kiss.

He rocked back, blinking.

"I can't do this. I can't. I thought I could." Tears sprang to her eyes and tumbled down her cheeks. "I'm so sorry." She wrenched the ring from her finger and pressed it into his palm. "This will never work. I should have known it the moment you put this ring on my finger, but I didn't want to believe it. I'm sorry." Knowing she'd made a fool of herself, tasting the bitterness of dashed hopes, she stumbled to her feet and ran to the house.

A last look over her shoulder showed Eli standing beside the garden bench, a bewildered expression on his face.

fifteen

Josie threw herself across her bed, sobs wracking her body. She cried from a place deep inside her heart, a place so secret she hadn't even known it existed. "God, I'm so sorry. Please help me."

She was barely aware of the mattress sinking down and someone smoothing her hair until Grandma Bess spoke. "There, there, child. It can't be that bad."

Josie pushed herself up and flung herself into Grandma's waiting arms. For long moments she cried, unable to stop, unable to catch her breath. When at last the tears were spent, she pulled back from Grandma's comforting embrace. Hiccups jerked her with every breath.

"All done?" Grandma leaned over the side of the bed and dug in her ever-present bag. "Here." She pressed a comfortingly large handkerchief into Josie's trembling hands. "Mop up a bit and we'll talk."

Josie sniffed and wiped her tears. "There's—" *Hiccup.* "There's nothing to talk about."

Grandma leveled an "oh really" look at her. "Then you're just wailing for the fun of it?"

Josie knew she'd have to tell Grandma something or she'd never let it rest. And suddenly, the chance to come clean, to confess everything and have her ragged feelings soothed seemed too good to pass up. "I gave Eli back his ring." Her heart tore afresh and another cascade of tears gushed down her cheeks.

"Oh? You aren't going to marry him then?"

She shook her head, balling up the handkerchief. "I can't."

132

"Did he say or do something horrible to you?" The placid expression on Grandma's face told Josie she wasn't particularly worried about Josie's answer.

"Of course not. His behavior was impeccable." His kiss lingered on her lips, a memory she would treasure forever.

"Then you discovered something about him that makes him unsuitable as a husband?"

"No. He would be a perfect husband." So far, Grandma's soothing left a little to be desired.

"Then you've decided he is unlovable."

"Stop it. I love him, and you know it or you wouldn't keep after me this way."

Grandma sighed and got up from the side of the bed. She settled herself in the rocking chair in the corner and placed her bag on her lap. "Let me get this straight. He has impeccable manners, is perfectly suitable as a husband, and you love him, yet you aren't going to marry him."

"That's right. I can't."

"Why not? It's plain as a porcupine you're made for one another."

"I can't marry him because he doesn't return my love. He doesn't even know the real me. I'll always be just the next Zahn girl on the list." Bitterness laced her words.

"What nonsense is this? The next Zahn girl on the list?"

"Clarice was his first choice, but she eloped. And I was next in line. Like we're interchangeable parts. One is as good as another. Just like Papa. He can't remember our names half the time."

"Josephine Zahn, I thought you had more sense. People think an old woman doesn't notice things, but that's not true. I see more than people give me credit for. Clarice was no more his first choice than he was hers. And I saw how Eli acted around Clarice, and I've seen how he acts around you. Believe me, he knows the difference. As for your father,

I suspect his forgetfulness regarding you girls is put on. He pretends with you. It's a game. Mark my words, young lady, Eli Kennebrae is in love with you. Even *he* might not know how much."

Josie hardly dared hope Grandma spoke the truth. Did he love her? Reality dragged her shoulders down. "But even if he does love me, I can't marry him. I'd be disobeying God."

Grandma blinked. "Disobeying God?"

Josie nodded. A strand of hair came loose out of her braid and clung to her damp cheek. "I've loved Eli for a long time. Right after Eli and Clarice became engaged, I promised God that instead of hankering after Eli I would be the woman He made me to be. I promised Him I would pursue His calling on my life to be an engineer. Then Clarice eloped and Eli proposed, and in a weak moment I accepted. I turned my back on my promise to God."

The way Grandma closed her eyes and moved her lips made Josie think she might be praying for patience. "Girl, you do get things in a snarl, don't you? How will marrying Eli keep you from being the woman God meant you to be? You think it is an either-or situation? And just because you promised something to God doesn't mean that was His will for you in the first place."

"But what about my abilities? If I marry Eli, I can't be an engineer. Men don't want wives who have careers. Geoffrey made that plain to me. That's why—" She broke off.

"That's why what? And what does Geoffrey have to do with anything?"

Josie twisted the soggy handkerchief, staring at her hands. Hot embarrassment flowed over her. "Eli has been corresponding with an engineer through Geoffrey. Someone who has been helping him with the designs for the *Bethany*." Her voice sounded small and faraway in her ears, like Giselle's when she was caught in some mischief. "I knew I could do the work, but

I knew no man would take me seriously because I'm a girl. So I made up an identity, a Professor Josephson, to work with Eli. All communication is run through Geoffrey. Eli thinks the professor is a recluse and a hermit. But"—she swallowed hard against the lump in her throat—"the professor is me."

A sigh as deep as Lake Superior came from Grandma's chest. "So you've done exactly what you promised God you wouldn't do. You've hidden your light under a bushel, to pull a verse out of context. You're not being the woman God made you to be, too scared to stand up and say you are a fine engineer. No wonder you can't see which way God wants you to go. You've been lying, both to Eli and to Him. If you harbor sin in your heart—sin you know and do nothing about—God isn't likely to answer your prayers."

Grandma's words, though said with love and gentle correction, still hit Josie like knife blades. "What should I do?"

"I think you know the answer to that, at least the first thing."

A giant hand of guilt pressed against Josie's chest. She nodded, unable to speak. She needed to confess her sin. Then, and only then, could she begin to hope God would show her what to do about Eli.

"As for what to do after that, I think you know that, too. You need to tell Eli the truth. You've sold him short. By lying to him and assuming he would scorn your engineering efforts, you haven't given him a chance to handle things well. I think you're underestimating Eli. And God. You've been so busy trying to figure everything out, to engineer what you thought was the right solution, you've eliminated the need for faith and trust. You haven't trusted God with your future, and you haven't trusted Eli with your abilities."

Grandma rose from the rocker, crossed the room, and sat beside Josie again, putting her comforting arms around Josie's shoulders and hugging her close. "You are so like me. Do you know how often I've let something that should be my greatest strength become my greatest weakness? God gave you the ability to design, to calculate, to figure. And applied to shipbuilding or architecture or mathematics, it's a fine gift. But when you start trying to engineer circumstances and people, design and force God's plan to be revealed to you, or construct your future the way you want it to be instead of the way God has for you, you run into trouble."

Josie leaned her head against her grandmother's soft shoulder, breathing in the smell of lemon verbena toilette water and talcum powder. "Do you think it is too late for Eli and me?"

"Give the young man a chance. You might be surprised."

⁂

Eli jammed his walking stick into the holder in the hall tree and smacked his hat onto a peg. The carpet on the stairs muffled his forceful footsteps in a totally unsatisfactory way. If he lived to be a thousand he would never understand women. One moment things were going well—laughing, talking, sharing deep secrets—and the next, *wham*! He was left alone in the garden holding a ring.

The feel of her in his arms, the rush of exultation when his lips met hers, the way her violet scent wrapped around him—all of it galled him. He'd been a fool to think she would accept his advances. And he blamed his grandfather as much as anyone. Grandfather had pushed him into the first engagement, held out promises to him. Then, when things looked like they were falling apart, he guilted Eli into another engagement with false claims of a bad heart. And Eli had allowed it like some dumb sheep.

He reached his bedroom and slammed the door. A sheaf of papers slid off a chair onto the floor. "If there was a prize for being a chump, I'd win, hands down."

"Is there a prize for being a chump?"

Eli spun toward the fireplace.

His brother Noah unfolded his long frame from the wing-back chair.

"Noah!"

"Hello, little brother."

Eli found himself in a bear hug that shoved the air from his chest. "Little brother, nothing," he gasped when Noah released him. "We're twins."

Noah cuffed him on the shoulder, his bearded face split in a wide grin. "But I was born first. Those few precious minutes make all the difference. But what's this about you being a chump?"

Eli shrugged. "Nothing out of the ordinary these days." He took Noah's measure. "Marriage agrees with you. You look. . . content."

Noah dropped back into his chair and stretched out his legs, lacing his fingers across his lean middle. "You're looking at a happy man. I highly recommend marital bliss, Eli. I understand you've jumped into the matrimonial pool, too."

"Humph. I thought I had, but apparently the pool is dry. The lady has rebuffed my advances, refused my suit, and given me back my ring. Though I'd just as soon you didn't tell Grandfather yet. I'll tell him later myself." He dug in his pocket and produced the offending bit of gold and gemstones. "And you know what she said? She should've known it wouldn't work the moment I put this ring on her finger." He tossed the ring to his brother.

Noah caught the ring and studied it, then glanced up at Eli, his eyes twinkling. "Well, that doesn't sound too promising. What are you going to do about it?"

"Do? What can I do? You can't argue with a returned ring. Just when I thought things were going well, she hands me the mitt and runs away. Women are a mystery well beyond my ability to solve."

"Now you sound like you're ready to get married. The moment you figure out that you'll never figure them out, you've got them figured out." Noah held up the diamonds to sparkle in the sunshine from the window.

"Make sense, will you? It's not funny." He snatched the ring back and stuffed it in his pocket.

Noah's grin faded and his eyes narrowed. "Say, you sound really hurt. Don't tell me you've fallen for this girl?"

Eli tried to bear up under Noah's scrutiny, his mind scrambling for an answer. He didn't have to search far. He knew his heart. He knew how he felt about Josie, how he'd felt about her from the moment he saw her at the wedding reception. "Well, what if I have? Maybe I'm no different than you and Jonathan. You both fell in love with the women Grandfather chose for you."

Noah leaned forward and tapped Eli on the side of the knee. "Hey, there's nothing wrong with it. In fact, it's wonderful. Like I said, marriage is the best thing that ever happened to me."

"You're forgetting the lady turned me down."

"I'll give you a little hint, Eli. Sometimes women say one thing and mean another."

"Why do they do that? It's like they expect you to read their minds. But if she didn't mean she wanted to end the engagement, what did she mean?"

"If you think this girl is worth it, little brother, then you should find out. That is, if you love her."

Eli sighed and raked his fingers through his hair. "I love her, and it's driving me crazy."

sixteen

Eli stalked across the sidewalk and entered the restaurant. Business. That's what he needed. He needed to focus on business and put matters of the heart aside for now. He crossed the dining room, weaving between tables, catching snippets of conversation as he headed toward the back corner.

Noon at The Black Horse, and every businessman on Minnesota Point could be found here. More deals were done over steak at The Black Horse than in the boardrooms of Duluth. The sound of cutlery and commerce flowed.

Geoffrey waved to him. At least his lawyer was on time.

Eli took his seat and ignored the menu. "Geoff, I want to know who the professor is and no more of your slippery evasions." If he couldn't solve one problem, he'd solve another. "Grandfather insists on meeting the man, and I want to issue an invitation for him to accompany us on the race. The designing engineers deserve to be in the pilothouse." He snapped open his napkin and spread it across his lap.

"Now, Eli, you know I can't do that. Why don't you just trust me when I say he can't and won't come?" Geoff's face disappeared behind his menu.

"There's something fishy about this whole situation. Where'd you meet this man anyway? If he never sees anyone, then why will he see you? And how did you just happen to pull an engineer out of your pocket at the precise moment I needed one? It isn't you, is it? Put that menu down so I can look you in the eye."

A waiter hovered, and Eli clenched his fists at the delay.

They placed their orders, and Geoffrey lifted his water

glass. "No"—he took a long swallow—"it isn't me. I wouldn't know the first thing about ship design."

"Then who is it? One of the college dons? I've checked. There is no Josephson on faculty at the college. In fact, there's no Josephsons that I can find anywhere in town."

"You've been looking?" Geoff's eyebrows rose.

"Of course I have, and so has Grandfather. And you know how thorough his investigations can be. But so far they've turned up nothing." Eli placed his palms flat on the table. "Geoff, why are you lying to me? And don't deny it. I know you are. There's something wrong about all of this. Josephson either doesn't exist or that isn't his real name."

Geoff looked at the ceiling. "If I could tell you, I would, but I'm not at liberty to say."

"That's convenient." Eli knew he was overreacting, but the sting of Josie's refusal and the frustration of knowing he'd have to face his grandfather with it goaded him on. "I took your elopement in stride, knowing it was for the best, and I even took your part when Grandfather wanted to fire you. And how do you repay me? By hiding behind your lawyer talk." He thumped the table, surprised at his own vehemence. "Tell me where to find Professor Josephson."

A hand whacked him on the shoulder. "Kennebrae, how are things?"

He looked up into the badgerish face of Gervase Fox. Every muscle in his jaw tightened. "Just fine."

"I couldn't help but overhear. You're looking for Professor Josephson?" The look in Fox's eye made Eli instantly wary.

"That's right. Do you know him?" Surely not.

"Of course I do, my boy. And so do you." A nasty grin split Fox's whiskers.

"Enough, Mr. Fox." Geoffrey put down his fork. "Stop with your jests. You don't know anything about this situation, and it is boorish of you to insinuate otherwise."

A flush climbed above Fox's beard. "Young man, I'm not jesting. Not only do I know the identity of Professor Josephson, but I've been in contact with said engineer. You should know. You're the one who introduced us, though I don't suppose you meant to at the time. I will say bumping into you two down at the canal was fortuitous for me. I was able to put two and two together and do a little investigating, and *presto!*"

As much as it galled him, Eli had to know. "Then tell me where to find him. He's done some collaborative work for me, and I wish to meet him face-to-face."

A laugh shook Fox's belly. "My dear boy, there is no Professor Josephson, at least not the academic you seem to think. Your assistant engineer is none other than your own fiancée, Josephine Zahn." Billows of raucous laughter nearly choked Gervase. "I can't believe you didn't know. Your lawyer knew, that's for certain. Look at him. He looks like he's swallowed a wasp."

Incredulity stunned Eli speechless. He looked from the beet red, guffawing Fox to Geoffrey's stricken face and knew Fox spoke the truth. Josie? An engineer?

When Fox regained his breath, he crossed his arms and leaned on the back of a vacant chair at their table. "I have to say, the 'professor's' designs are quite revolutionary. And they're good, too. Just to be sure of her ability, I had her teacher tracked down at his new employment in Detroit. Though my investigator couldn't get much out of the man, his students are known for their engineering abilities, and I've found no reason why Josephine should be any different. Her drawings are quite amazing. She's been quite good to work with." He wiped his eyes. "And your trying so hard to keep me out of your shipyard so I wouldn't see them, when I've had the information all the while."

Eli found his voice. "Josie's Professor Josephson? She's

been giving you my ship plans all along?" His heart squeezed in a giant vise.

"Of course. Why do you think I was so quick to entice your grandfather into this match race? I never would've taken the chance otherwise, not if you truly had a secret design that might best me." Fox stood upright and hooked his thumbs in his vest pockets.

She'd lied to him. Lied to him and betrayed him. Everything he thought about her, everything he thought she stood for, that he thought she might feel for him, that he felt for her, underwent a radical change.

"Don't take it too hard, boy. You've just had a taste of the cutthroat world of business. You'll get used to it." Fox clapped him on the shoulder, but Eli barely felt it.

"I think you'd better leave." Geoff stood up and stepped forward. "You've said far too much."

"And you haven't said enough. If I found out my lawyer was lying to me the way you lie to the Kennebraes, he'd not only be unemployed, I'd run him right out of town." Fox dug in his pocket for a cigar. "The only way to win in business is to look out for yourself. You can't be afraid to get your hands dirty. You'll both learn, though, some lessons come harder than others." He struck a match with his thumbnail and disappeared behind a puffing cloud of cigar smoke.

"Get out." Eli stood up. "You've had your fun, now leave." His gut muscles clenched so hard his body shook. He wanted to bury his fist in Fox's smug face, drive that cigar down his throat.

Fox barked with laughter. "Fine. I'll go. Give my regards to Josie." He waved his cigar and strode through the dining room, head back, still laughing.

Eli eased into his chair. Every eye in the place was on him, and the diners had heard at least part of the exchange with Fox. The only sound was the door closing behind Fox's retreating form.

Geoff looked across at him, his eyes clouded.

Slowly conversations picked up, forks scraped against china, and men turned their attention away from Eli's table.

"It's true, isn't it?"

Geoff nodded.

"Why?" One flat word, a single question that both asked for an explanation and accused his friend for his duplicity.

"Eli, it isn't as bad as you think." Geoff spread his hands in a placating gesture.

"I don't want any of your lawyer talk. I want the straight truth, not that I'll be able to trust it coming from you." A thrust of satisfaction charged through Eli when Geoff winced and dropped his gaze. "Why would you do this to me? Why would Josie?"

"At first we did it to stall. But after, we were both in so deep, and it seemed to be working, so we kept it up."

"Stall? Stall what?"

"Just hear me out." Geoff straightened his spine. "You were going to marry my girl, and I was desperate to find a way to stall your marriage and get her out of there. I knew you weren't keen on the situation, and you only wanted to work on the *Bethany*. I figured if I could keep your attention on your work, I'd have time to find a solution that would free Clarice. I knew you needed an engineer, and Clarice and Josie assured me Josie could do the work. But since she's a girl, she didn't think you'd listen to her ideas. So we dreamed up Professor Josephson." His eyes telegraphed his misery, but he didn't look away. "This is all my fault. Don't blame Josie."

"Don't blame her? After she's been duping me? And not only that, but giving my ideas to Fox? To *Fox* of all people?" Eli wasn't sure which hurt the worst, betrayal by his friend, his fiancée, or his foe. No, that wasn't true. Josie's betrayal hurt the worst.

"You can't believe anything Fox says." Geoff pushed back

his nearly full plate and put his elbows on the table.

"Unlike you and Josie, who are models of truthfulness?" Sarcasm soaked his tone. "How else would he know her identity? Why else would he be so cocksure he would win the race?"

Geoffrey rammed his fingers into his hair. "I don't know how he knew. He's slippery. But Josie wouldn't have shared the information with him. She knew how sensitive it was. She knew how much it meant to you. How much it meant to her."

"If she knew and told him anyway, that makes it worse."

"Go talk to her. Find out how this happened."

"Forget it." Eli's heart went hard as a chunk of ice. She'd handed back her ring because she knew she'd betrayed him and she couldn't stomach it. "If Fox has implemented the same designs as the *Bethany*, then the race will be closer than I thought. I have more than enough work to do without confronting Josie with her duplicity." He stood and scooted his chair under the table.

For a long moment he looked down on the man he had thought was his best friend. "I don't know what I'll tell Grandfather. If I tell him the truth, he'll have you cleaning out your office in the Kennebrae Building before supper. I don't think you meant me any harm with your lying, but it's harmed me all the same. Just stay away from me from now on."

seventeen

"But how did Fox find out?" Despair clawed up Josie's throat.

Geoff stood before her, mangling his hat brim. "I don't know. He mentioned meeting us together near the canal, and he said he'd had you checked out, sent an investigator to your tutor. Fox knew it all. He claimed you've been feeding him information all along, that he knows all the designs and modifications to the *Bethany*, and he's sure he can win the race. Threw it right into Eli's face."

"That's impossible. The designs have never left my room unless they were in your possession. Every time you brought me new plans, I took them right up to my desk." Josie sank onto the garden bench, the same bench where only two days before Eli had held her in his arms. "What did Eli say?"

"He walked out like he was in a trance. I went back to the office, but he wasn't in the Kennebrae Building. I don't know where he is. I decided I'd better head over here in case he'd come to confront you about things."

"Did he fire you?" Guilt at landing Geoffrey in so much trouble swamped her.

"No, but as good as. When Abraham finds out what we've been up to, he'll sack me for sure."

Josie blinked back tears and twisted her fingers. "Grandma Bess was right. She says a lie that goes on only gets more and more complicated until the liar is tied up in her own web. I'm so sorry, Geoff. I never should've drawn you into this."

"Don't take all the blame for yourself. I had a major hand in this." Geoff paced the flagstone path. "That still doesn't explain how Fox knew. If you didn't tell him, and I certainly didn't, then how would he get his hands on the plans? What about a servant? Could a maid have slipped him the information?"

"No, we don't have an upstairs maid for the bedrooms. Mama thinks we girls should care for our own rooms the way she had to."

"Are any of the plans missing?"

"No, that's just it. I've got them all. When I'm done with the papers, I either give them to you or I burn them in the stove."

Something tickled the back of Josie's mind, and she stopped speaking to focus on it. Something about Fox and her room. . . She shook her head. Grasping at straws. "What do you think Eli will do?"

Geoff stopped pacing and fixed his gaze on her face. "Clarice says you're in love with Eli. That you've loved him for a long time. Is that true?"

Josie closed her eyes against the wave of pain and loss that crashed over her. Unable to speak around the lump in her throat, she could only nod. When she composed herself, she whispered, "It doesn't matter now. He won't even talk to me. He'll never be mine. I broke the engagement two days ago. And he'd never take me back, not believing I betrayed him."

Geoff sank down on the bench beside her and put his arm around her in a brotherly hug. "I'm so sorry, Josie. But don't give up yet. We'll think of something."

☙

"I'm not surprised she broke the engagement. The last shred of her conscience must've goaded her into it. Couldn't face marrying you when she'd lied." Grandfather edged his chair farther into Eli's shipyard workroom.

"I don't want to talk about it." Eli spread a map on the table. "Noah, now that you've been over the ship, what do you think of her?"

Noah leaned against the wall, arms crossed, one ankle over the other. "I'd hardly recognize her if her name wasn't painted on the stern. You've done a remarkable job with the repairs."

"And I think you'll find she handles well, too. I wish we had time to give her a thorough shakedown before the race, but we'll just have time to get her launched and fueled before next week. The hatches will be done in a few more days. Those gaskets were harder to fashion than I anticipated."

"Don't you ignore me, young man." Grandfather poked Eli in the side. "I came down here to talk about Josie, so start talking."

"She broke the engagement. That's all there is to say. Now leave it. I'm busy." He pointed to the map. "Noah, you'll load here at the Zahn number two dock in Two Harbors. The cranes are being erected up there right now to lower the units into the hold. I've had to reinforce the pilings to accommodate the extra weight." He leafed through the large papers on the desk and withdrew the plan for the loading system. "No more shoving one board at a time into the hold. You can be loaded in under four hours. I guarantee it."

Noah gave a low whistle of appreciation. "Four hours to load a lumber ship. It's unheard of."

"We have to assume Fox has this plan. He's taken over Zahn's number one dock, and from what I can tell, he's making much the same adjustments over there to crane load." Eli ground his teeth.

"I'm sorry about that." Noah shook his head. "It's a shame your girl let you down like that."

Grandfather snorted. "Thick as thieves, Fox and those Zahns. You made a lucky escape, boy. Radcliffe turned on me over the shipping contracts, and that girl betrayed you to our rival."

Eli slammed his pencil down with a slap. "I said I'm through talking about this. If you'd minded your own business instead of trying to shove me into an engagement I never wanted in the first place *and* if you'd have kept your mouth shut when Fox showed up at that picnic, I wouldn't be in this mess. As usual, you leap first and think later. Now, unless you want to back out of this race and just hand the *Bethany* over to Fox right now, I suggest you leave me alone to finish the repairs." He turned to his brother. "I'll be back when the room is a little less crowded."

The entire shack shuddered when he slammed the door, but he didn't care. Grandfather could stew in his own juice. From now on, Eli was his own man. He'd do his best to win this race, for his brothers' sakes and Kennebrae Shipping, but after that, he was finished.

Good shipbuilders were needed back East. If he couldn't get hired on somewhere, he'd start his own company. And he'd stay away from women, lawyers, and interfering old men.

eighteen

Josie braced herself against the concrete pier wall, leaning out over the canal.

People pushed and shoved, trying to find good spots from which to see the race. In the background, the Duluth City Band played a lively tune. Bunting and flags flapped in the gusting wind.

She glanced up at the swollen, tumbling clouds that looked ready to burst with rain at any moment. What should've been a glorious day hovered, anxious and out of sorts, much like Josie herself.

Whitecaps and chop slapped against the pier side, sucking and slurping as if trying to climb over each other to get onshore. She pulled her coat tight.

"Is it time?" Giselle tugged on Josie's hand. "When will the boats come?"

"I told you, wait for the whistle. The ships will pull out of their docks and head right through the canal. You won't miss a thing."

Josie put her hand on Toni's shoulder and tugged her back. "The race will be irrelevant to you if you plunge into that cold water. And Mama will have a fit."

Toni rolled her eyes but kept her heels on the ground.

Giselle yanked on Josie's sleeve. "I wish we could ride on the boat like Papa. Why'd he go on Mr. Fox's boat? I thought he would ride with Eli. That's where I'd go. I like Eli better. Mr. Fox thinks little girls are stupid. But he's the one who is stupid." She stuck out her tongue and crossed her eyes. "He couldn't even find the washroom when he was at our house, even though I told him where it was. He went right into your room instead. Stupid man."

Josie grabbed Giselle by the shoulders. "Mr. Fox was in my room? You saw him? When?"

The little girl blinked, her lower lip quivering. "I didn't do anything wrong. I promise."

Josie loosened her grip. "It's all right, Giselle. You're not in trouble. But you're sure you saw Mr. Fox in my room?"

The little girl's black curls bounced when she nodded. "He was in there a long time. That's why I thought he was stupid. He should've known right off that wasn't the washroom."

Josie's lips pressed tight in vindication. Fox *had* gone into her room and stolen the plans. Her shoulders sagged. Little good it would do her, though. If Eli wouldn't listen to her, he wasn't likely to listen to Giselle.

A whistle blast pierced the air, quickly swallowed by the shouts around her. The race was on!

Josie pressed her middle against the seawall and leaned out as far as she dared, trying to see past the heads and shoulders of others doing the same. Her hands pressed the concrete, her palms stinging.

The *Keystone Vulpine* appeared first, riding high, the water churning to foam in her wake. Almost in her shadow, the *Bethany* nosed forward. The *Vulpine* would make it out of Duluth Harbor first. The ship passed before them, stack belching smoke, cutting through the green blue water with ease. High above the crowd, deckhands lined the rail.

"There's Papa! Look, Josie, it's Papa!" Giselle hopped, clapping and waving by turns.

Radcliffe Zahn stood in the pilothouse doorway, the lapels of his greatcoat fluttering.

Josie tore her gaze away, disappointment at her father's actions coursing through her. That he would treat his agreement with the Kennebraes so cavalierly, aligning himself with their rival while still expecting them to honor the engagement between the families, shamed her. His claim that it was "just business" and she "wouldn't understand" didn't cut much ice with Josie. The way a person conducted business revealed character. She hoped he would be as cavalier when she told him of the broken engagement.

She swallowed. She hadn't conducted her business very well. What did that say about her character?

The *Vulpine*'s midship glided past. Josie concentrated on the hull. A converted ore carrier just like the *Bethany*. She knew the hold would contain the same storage and loading apparatus as Eli had designed. The interior bracing, the hull dimensions, all of it stolen by Fox. She closed her eyes and could see in her mind the final drawings—every line, every curve, every calculation clear. When she opened her eyes, the stern of the *Vulpine* slid past.

But something was different. Josie concentrated on the aft hatch cover, the ship's propulsion shortening her angle of view. The housing around the hatch looked odd. The shadow line seemed off somehow. A wide-brimmed hat blocked her vision.

Josie stepped back from the crowd lining the waterway and grabbed Giselle's and Toni's hands. She shouldered her way up the pier toward the open lake. A wild elbow dislodged her hat, but she ignored it and moved on, trying to get a better look at the departing ship.

A man caught her by the arm. "Whoa there, miss, what's your hurry?" A pair of field glasses swung from a strap around his neck.

"Please, sir, might I borrow those?" She released Toni's hand. "Stay right by me."

He smiled, clearly bemused, and took off his hat to remove the glasses.

She snatched them and pressed them to her eyes. The

Vulpine's stern leaped close in her vision. The ship quartered slightly, but even that angle presented her enough of a view to know she hadn't been wrong.

Fox's ship was a bomb waiting to go off. The hinges fastening the hatches to the deck were the same ones Eli had originally intended to use. If Fox had used the drawings from her desk the day he had visited the house, then those hinges were under-engineered. They'd facilitate the loading, but in bad weather, with the tremendous strain of water crashing over the deck, they'd let go.

The *Bethany* plunged through the Duluth Canal, her steel bulk obliterating the *Vulpine* from view. Josie swung the glasses upward and trained them on the pilothouse. Dark silhouettes moved in the little room. A face appeared in the window. A lump formed in her throat when she made out Eli's features. Then he was gone, the *Bethany* taking him out onto the lake.

Abraham Kennebrae. He was the only one with the clout to call a halt to the race before it was too late. But where in this throng could she find him?

The Kennebrae Building. She pressed the glasses back into the stranger's hand, flashed him a smile, and snaked through the crowd, dragging her sisters along in her wake. Thanks to the Duluth papers, the race had brought throngs of people down to the canal. By the time she reached the steps of the Kennebrae Shipping headquarters, she was out of breath. The comparative quiet of the lobby wrapped around her.

"May I help you, miss?" A sour-faced man behind a counter fixed her with a fishy eye, and his mouth pinched tight at sight of her little sisters gaping at the ornate interior of the office building. "There are no public facilities here. You'll have to go up the street."

"I came to see Mr. Abraham Kennebrae. Is he here?" Josie squared her shoulders and took a step forward.

"The offices are closed to business." His narrow nostrils twitched.

"If he is here, I must see him." She smoothed her wild hair, knowing it must look as if she'd combed it with a broom.

The watchdog stepped out from behind his oak and marble barricade. "Miss, I'm going to have to ask you to leave. Mr. Kennebrae doesn't have time for casual callers. Reporters have been trying to gain access all day."

"I'm not a reporter." Josie's eyes widened. "Please, you've got to let me see him."

"Dawkins? Is there a problem?" Jonathan Kennebrae came down the staircase. His stern expression blew frost over Josie's hopes. "What can I do for you?"

"I need to see Mr. Kennebrae right away."

Jonathan's brown eyes looked her up and down. "He won't welcome you. He's very angry about what you did, giving Eli's designs to Fox." He crossed his arms.

"But I didn't! And I can prove it. Please, I have to see him. He's the only one who can help me." She clasped his arm, pleading with him.

He blew out a breath and shook his head, and for a moment Josie feared he wouldn't help her. Finally, he shrugged. "Come along then."

Dawkins retreated, head bowed.

Josie just avoided sending a triumphant glance his way as she took Jonathan's arm and allowed him to lead her upstairs. She looked back over her shoulder to make sure Giselle and Toni followed.

Jonathan escorted them through a door at the end of a long hallway.

Once inside Abraham Kennebrae's sanctum, the words clogged in her throat. He perched in his chair like a bird of prey, the sweeping views of the lake spreading before him. In the distance, the ships receded, steaming north to Two

Harbors. Lightning split the sky, and the windows rattled with the crack of thunder that followed. As if the sound had burst the bottom of the clouds open, rain spattered the glass then sluiced down in a blurry sheet.

"Josephine." He turned hawk eyes toward them, so intense under lowered white brows her courage nearly deserted her. "Have you come to crow? Selling us out to Gervase Fox. Do you have any idea what you've done to Eli? What you've done to Kennebrae Shipping?" Though Jonathan made tamping down motions with his hands, Abraham stormed on. "You Zahns are turning out to be a rum lot."

"Mr. Kennebrae. . ." Her voice sounded small in the cavernous room. But she forged on, seeing again her father's profile on the deck of the *Vulpine*. Panic clawed her insides, forcing the words out though she wanted to flee his accusations. "Mr. Kennebrae, you have to stop this race."

He blinked and sat back.

She rushed on. "Fox's ship is unsafe. The hatches won't stand up to the strain, especially in a storm. I know you think I betrayed Eli, but I didn't. Mr. Fox stole the plans of the *Bethany* from my room." She turned to Giselle and drew the little girl forward. "Tell him what you told me about Mr. Fox."

Giselle took one look at Abraham and clamped her mouth shut. She gripped Josie's hand and lowered her chin, looking at the old man through her lashes.

"Please, Giselle, it's important."

"No, he's mean. He talked mean to you, Josie."

"I'll tell." Toni stepped forward, her hands on her hips. "That sneaky Mr. Fox came to our house pretending to be nice to Mama. But he wasn't really nice. He said he needed to use the washroom, but he didn't. He snuck into Josie's room and was in there a long, long time. That's where Josie keeps all her papers and drawings, all the stuff from helping Eli build his ship. And I think it's rotten of you to say Josie sold you out to Mr. Fox. She doesn't even like him. She'd never do anything to hurt Eli. She loves Eli."

Heat raced up Josie's cheeks.

Abraham looked up at her then returned his gaze to Toni. "She does, does she? And what makes you say that?"

"She's worked so hard on his plans. And she gets all dreamy after he visits, and I saw her kiss him in our garden. She wouldn't kiss him if she didn't love him."

Josie's humiliation was complete. If only she could evaporate right then.

Abraham fixed her with another sharp look. "That makes excellent sense, young lady. Now, tell me again about Mr. Fox."

Toni's hands came off her hips at his softened tone, and she edged forward, reciting once more how Mr. Fox had gone into Josie's room and looked through the papers on her desk.

"Josie, is there a problem with Fox's ship?" Jonathan cocked his head to the side.

"He took the plans from my room before I figured out the solution to the hatch flaw that had been plaguing Eli from the first. Fox has used the previous design, and it won't hold in rough seas. It might not give way during the race, but if any water comes over the bow, at best the hatches will leak, at worst they'll give way altogether."

She snatched a piece of paper off the desk and hastily sketched a few lines. "This is the old design. Unless he changed the specifications, they'll never hold. And here"— she scratched a rough outline—"is the new design. It's based upon a railroad coupling design, and it's much stronger. The rubber gasket paired with the new hatch closure will ensure a watertight seal."

Abraham, holding Toni's hand now, shook his head. "That's Fox's worry. Serves him right for stealing the plans in the first place."

"But Papa's on that ship." Giselle spoke up at last. "Is it going to sink?"

Jonathan knelt beside the little girl. "No, honey. Don't you worry. They'll be fine." He looked over her shoulder to his grandfather. "We'll see that your papa is safe. Won't we, Grandfather?"

Abraham scowled then motioned to the girls. "Why don't you girls check in the bottom drawer of my desk? There's a box in there. You can have whatever you like. Your sister and I are going to go out. Jonathan?" Abraham jerked his head toward the door. "Get someone to stay with the little girls then come downstairs."

Josie followed Mr. Kennebrae down the hall, his chair making no noise on the carpet. They entered a small elevator, and the old man pulled the lever for the first floor. "The ships are too far from shore to contact and stop. We'll have to see if we can intercept them while they're loading at Two Harbors." He shot out of the elevator across the lobby.

"By ship? Do you have a launch that can make it there so quickly?" Josie trotted after him.

"Not by ship. We'll go by motorcar up the Vermillion Trail." He snapped his fingers and the watchdog by the door jerked to attention. "Get the car. . .and hurry."

nineteen

The ride up the North Shore was an adventure Josie would not soon forget. Exponentially more hair-raising than the gondola ride across the Duluth Channel. She bounced and bucked on the seat as scrub trees, rocks, and brief glimpses of the lake flashed by.

The driver, trench-coated and leather-gloved, took his employer at his word and kept the vehicle—a brand-new Oldsmobile—rocketing along the road. Rain poured down and the wind howled off the water.

Several times on the journey, Jonathan turned to check on her from the front seat. Each time she tried to raise a smile and nod.

When the sturdy red brick lighthouse at Two Harbors rose before them and they bumped along the street toward the docks, Josie wanted to cry with relief. Both the *Vulpine* and the *Bethany* sat at the docks while two steam cranes loaded their gaping holds.

The car stopped at the end of the dock and Josie shot out, not waiting for the Kennebraes.

The *Vulpine* sat closest to her, a group of men clustered around the crane. Fox strutted between the piles of lumber, pointing and directing traffic. Papa stood to one side, clutching an umbrella and observing the loading.

As she approached him, she looked over the side, fighting a bit of dizziness as a bundle swung from the end of the crane and into the hold far below. "Papa, I have to speak with you."

He gaped at her as if she had appeared out of the air. "What are you doing here, girl? And how'd you get here?"

"Papa, please, there isn't time. We need to stop the race and get the *Vulpine* home safely. Stop the loading. The more she's loaded, the worse the problem will become. She'll ride lower in the water and increase the likelihood that waves will break over the deck."

"Stop talking nonsense, Josephine. I know you fancy yourself some kind of engineer." He rolled his eyes. "It's my fault for letting your grandmother fill your head with nonsense. But you've no business butting in here. Fox has things well in hand. He'll win this race without too much trouble. We were in well ahead of the *Bethany*, and the loading's almost finished."

"It isn't nonsense, Papa. Please listen to me." She tugged at his arm, feeling as young as Giselle. "The ship isn't sound."

Abraham Kennebrae rolled near them, Jonathan right behind. "Listen to her, Radcliffe. We have to stop the race. Where's Fox?"

Fox rounded a stack of white pine. "I should've known you'd show up here. You've all but lost the race, Kennebrae. I'll be loaded and out of here in less than an hour."

"Mr. Fox, I know you stole the plans from my room." Josie clutched her coat closed at her throat and braced herself against the strong wind. "But you stole them too early. The hatch design you used won't hold in this weather. Especially when you're loading her so heavily. She'll have almost no freeboard if you fill her holds."

Fox ignored her words and sneered at Abraham. "Do you think I'm a fool? This is just another effort on your part to get me to lose this race. It won't work. I'm going to win, and the *Bethany* will belong to me."

No amount of arguing would change his mind, and Josie's father stood firm no matter how she pled with him.

"Let's go see Eli." Abraham pointed up the dock to the *Bethany*. "At the very least he should know to watch out."

The moment Josie dreaded now stared her in the face. She followed the Kennebraes down the dock, head down into the wind. Rain pounded across the dock and shocked her with its chill.

"Grandfather?" Eli spun on his heel when Abraham called out to him. "Jonathan? How did you get here?"

"Never mind that. Let's get out of this rain. We need to talk." Abraham rolled his chair toward the gangplank of the *Bethany*, and Jonathan grabbed the bar along the back to keep him from rolling off the side.

Eli turned to follow then froze. "Josie?" The incredulity and accusation in his eyes made her wish she'd never come.

જ

Why had she come? To gloat? To see for herself how the *Vulpine* fared against the *Bethany*? Eli had every confidence that Noah would best the *Vulpine* captain with a loaded boat in high seas. If Josie had come to lord it over him, she would be sorely disappointed.

Wind-whipped rain plastered her uncovered hair. She implored him with her eyes, her look slicing through him.

He quelled the rush of caring that rose over him. He knew a desire to shelter her from the elements, to take her into his arms. But she had betrayed him. Deceived him. His guard must remain firmly in place. "What do you want?" He kept his voice as cold as the rain.

"Eli, please, I know you're angry with me, but I had to come see Fox."

He turned away from her, the pain of her betrayal too great. From her own mouth she admitted coming to see Fox? "He's over there. Why come down here?" He pulled the collar of his oilskin higher. "No doubt he'll welcome you with open arms."

She shoved him hard enough to make him take a step to the side. "Stop being so thickheaded. I came because the

Vulpine isn't seaworthy. It's the hatches."

He looked down into her face, streaked with rain and pinched with cold. A sodden lock of hair lay plastered to her pale cheek.

She grasped his forearm, her grip fierce. "Please, Eli, won't you listen? I know you think I betrayed you, and in a way, by lying about being Professor Josephson, I did. I'm sorry." She shook her head, remorse lining her brow. "But I didn't give your designs to Fox. He stole them. He got into my room and took the plans."

"No more lies, Josie." He disengaged her hand from his arm. "If you would lie about being an engineering professor, you'd lie about anything." A bitter taste coated his tongue and flowed down to flavor his heart.

Jonathan and Abraham appeared on the deck. A shout went up from a longshoreman near the crane.

Eli stepped back and pointed to the shore. "We're loaded. Go back to Duluth with Grandfather. I want to put this entire farce behind me."

"But, Eli, please. You have to listen to me. The *Vulpine*—"

Her pleading, and the fact that he felt himself weakening against it, irked him. "Don't talk to me about Fox or his ship. Just go."

Her shoulders drooped, and her chin went down. He couldn't be sure, but he thought a pair of tears mingled with the rain coursing down her cheeks.

His hands reached for her, but he stopped them in time. No, she wouldn't sway him with tears.

Jonathan pushed Grandfather's chair down the gangplank. Eli's oldest brother looked at Josie's defeated frame. His eyebrows shot down, and he glared at Eli. "Josie?"

She sniffed and shook her head, then turned and walked up the dock toward the shore.

Jonathan turned to Eli. "What did you do to her?"

Anger exploded in red bursts on the edge of Eli's vision. "What did I do to *her*?" He gestured in a wide arc. "Why is it that no one seems to care about what she did to me? She lied to me. She betrayed me, and she might've cost me this race."

Grandfather motioned for Jonathan to push his chair on. "Let's not waste time on this hardheaded goat. Get aboard, Eli, and get out of here. We've talked to Noah. He knows what to watch for, and *he* didn't doubt a word we said."

Eli didn't wait for them to leave. He stalked up the gangway and stormed into the pilothouse. The deck hands winched the last hatch cover into place and spun the wheels to tighten the gaskets. Josie's gaskets.

Noah settled into the tall captain's chair. The helmsman lounged against the front windows, waiting for the signal to move out. But it didn't come.

"What are you waiting for? Cast off the lines." Eli stuck his head back out the door to where the *Vulpine* was throwing off lines and preparing to leave the dock. "Hurry up. You're losing time."

Noah frowned at him, puzzlement clouding his eyes. "We're leaving second. Didn't you talk to Josie?"

"I talked to her all right. Not that it did her any good. She lied to me and sold me out. Nothing she can say will alter those facts. But we're going to win despite her betrayal. Now, cast off." Eli gripped the doorframe, every muscle tight.

Noah's eyes narrowed, appraising Eli. "What about those hatches? If we pull out ahead of them, we won't be able to keep an eye on them. I promised Grandfather and Jonathan we'd stick close in case Fox's crew needed help."

The *Vulpine*'s whistle sounded. She steamed by with the help of a tug, Fox's face grinning triumphantly from the pilothouse window, Radcliffe Zahn at his shoulder.

Panic seized Eli. "Hurry up! Cast off!" he yelled at the crewmen on the catwalk below the pilothouse. "Shove off!"

Noah rose and stood nose to nose with Eli. "Belay that order, helm. We'll wait until they clear the harbor. I'm the captain of this ship. You don't give orders to my crew."

"Then you do it. We're going to lose this race with your lying about. Don't you care that we might lose the *Bethany*? Don't you care that Fox will gloat and crow, that he and Josie will have duped us from start to finish?" Eli grabbed Noah's lapels. "She lied to me!" This truth scored him more deeply than anything else. Even losing the race wouldn't hurt as badly as losing his ability to trust Josie.

Noah gripped Eli's wrists. "Get ahold of yourself. Take a good look at that ship. Jonathan says Fox stole the plans for the *Bethany* from Josie's room, but he did it before she fixed the hatch problem. She's not seaworthy." He ripped Eli's hands from his coat. "We're going to follow them to make sure they get to port safely. In these seas and loaded like she is—" He broke off and returned to his seat. "Cast off the bowline."

The helmsman signaled to the dock, and the heavy ropes securing the ship fell away.

Noah dialed the chadburn to quarter speed, the familiar bell jangling through the room.

Eli pressed his hand against the window, staring after the *Vulpine*. He lifted the field glasses from the rack on the wall and brought the hatches near in his vision. Righteous indignation clogged his throat.

He turned the dial to sharpen the focus. The *Bethany* shuddered under his feet, shouldering away from the dock and thrusting forward through the chop of the bay. Pin hinges. The same pin hinges he'd wrestled with for weeks. The view began to shake, and he realized he was gripping the field glasses so hard his fingers trembled.

"All ahead full." Noah dialed the chadburn again.

The helmsman repeated the order with the obligatory "sir" tacked on the end.

"Did you see it?" The captain's question was directed at Eli.

"Yes, I saw it."

"Well?"

Eli returned the field glasses to the rack. Guilt raced up his arms and across his chest, pressing against him. All the accusations he'd hurled at Josie slammed through his head. "She was telling the truth."

"How do you know?" Noah's voice goaded Eli, taunting him, pushing him to admit things he didn't want to. "You said she lied to you."

Eli whirled around, his hands fisted, legs braced apart. "I know her. She would never put people in danger. She would never have given Fox that hatch closure design. She's the one who convinced me it was flawed in the first place."

"What about the professor bit?" Noah's eyes drilled Eli.

Eli made an impatient gesture. "That didn't bother me as much as the thought of her selling out to Fox. Imagine what it must be like to be a girl with those skills. Would you have taken her seriously if she'd come right out and admitted she wanted to be an engineer?"

Noah gave a low command to the helmsman then shook his head. "No. It never would've occurred to me that a woman could be so gifted. And that's no credit to me." He stroked his beard. "Melissa and Annie would have both our hides."

A smile quirked Eli's mouth in response. "I think Josie will fit in quite nicely with the Kennebrae brides, don't you?"

Noah quirked his eyebrow. "Little brother," he drawled out the jibe, "that particular ship has run aground. Your engagement needs a refit. Grandfather said they'd be waiting at Kennebrae House, and he'd make sure Josie was there."

❧

Eli bounded up the steps of Kennebrae House, shedding his coat and tossing it to McKay, not waiting for Noah or Radcliffe Zahn to climb out of the automobile.

"They're in the gallery, sir," McKay called after him. "Congratulations."

Eli waved a hand in acknowledgment and strode down the hall. When he entered the art gallery, he stopped at the sight of so many people in the room. The guests assembled applauded and clapped him on the back, shaking his hand.

"Well done, my boy." Grandfather edged forward in his chair.

"Thank you, sir. The *Bethany* is docked and unloaded."

"The messenger you sent from the dock told us you rescued the crew of the *Vulpine* before she went down. Heard Fox gave you a rough time. If he keeps it up, we'll sic Geoffrey on him and sue him for defamation."

A long buffet table stretched down the center of the room, with a splashing punch fountain, ice sculptures, and the best of the Kennebrae larder. People smiled and laughed, talking and eating, celebrating the Kennebrae victory.

Though this should've been the happiest moment of Eli's life, the pinnacle of his hopes and dreams for his design and his place in the Kennebrae family, he felt no joy. The past twenty hours, since Josie had walked away from him on the Two Harbors dock, had been the longest of his life. The rescue, the return trip, the unloading, a thousand-and-one details to see to, but nothing could crowd out the memory of her stricken expression when he'd rebuffed her and refused to listen.

Octavia Zahn rushed past him to cast herself into her husband's arms, clinging to him. Zahn bore it stoically, patting her shaking shoulder awkwardly, staring at the pipe organ, as if waiting for her to pull herself together. She did manage to gather herself but continued to dab at her eyes with a handkerchief and to hang on Zahn's arm. The little Zahn girls clustered around. But Josie wasn't among them.

Jonathan pressed a glass of punch into Eli's hand. "Well done, little brother. I'm proud of you."

Eli flicked a glance at his brother, nodding his thanks for the compliment, but continued to scan the room for the face he sought. His eyes rested on Melissa, her arms cradling Matthew, face serene. Noah, standing next to her, had Annie tucked into his side, his arm around her waist. The baby seemed fascinated with Noah's whiskers, staring round-eyed and somber into his uncle's face. Grandfather sat near the massive fireplace. Above him, a heavy gilt frame surrounded his favorite painting, an oil of the family yacht, *The Lady Genevieve*, skimming the waves of Lake Superior on a sun-drenched day.

"Nice job, Eli." Geoffrey slid through the crowd to shake Eli's hand. Clarice joined them, tucking her hand into Geoff's elbow. Geoff bent a smile down at her.

Eli's heart twisted with envy, wanting Josie so bad it made his chest ache. Though Grandfather had assured Noah she would be here waiting for their return, he hadn't spotted her in the crowd yet.

Jonathan nudged Eli. "Tell me about the rescue."

Eli shrugged. "The *Vulpine*'s hatches started taking on water, just like Josie said they would, and the bilge pumps couldn't keep up. About halfway to harbor, the forward hatch hinge pins broke loose. She listed hard, taking on water. Noah launched the lifeboat, and we rescued the crew. The *Vulpine* went down, and Fox is livid."

"He's got no one to blame but himself. Do you think she's salvageable?" Jonathan tasted his punch, made a face, and set it on a passing tray.

"If she didn't hit too hard on the lake floor, but it's pretty deep there," Eli answered absently, his chest churning. Where was she?

Then he saw her.

For a moment his heart stopped cold. . .then took up banging like pots in a ship's galley in a gale.

In the light of the electric lamps Grandfather had turned on to supplement the gaslight, her skin took on a porcelain delicacy. Her eyes looked enormous and sad. She stood a little apart, her attention decidedly away from where Eli stood. She twisted the middle fingers of her left hand with her right. And he saw the bare left ring finger.

Guilt stabbed him again. He thrust his punch cup into Jonathan's hand. "Hold this, I'll be right back." He took the stairs two at a time and jogged down the hallway to his room. The box sat right where he'd left it. He snatched it up and hurried back to the gallery on the first floor.

His heart beat fast when he spotted her again. He started toward her, but Grandfather's voice stopped him.

"Eli, come here. Speech!" The old man's voice rang out strong and imperious.

Heart trouble, my eye. He tried to ignore the call, skirting well-wishers, but the guests took up the chant. "Speech! Speech!"

Josie edged toward the door.

He needed to get to her before she left. Then he knew what he had to do.

❧

Josie again declined punch from the servant circulating. She couldn't eat or drink anything, not with the steel hawsers clamping around her middle.

Eli had ducked out of the party, after standing beside his brother and sipping punch like he hadn't a care in the world. She told herself she didn't care where he'd gone. He skidded into the room and looked from face to face as if searching for someone.

A sob surprised her, hiccupping out before she could squelch it. The room closed in, people and noise pressing against her until she couldn't stand it anymore. Solace and quiet were only a few steps away. She could slip out and no one would notice.

A hand closed over her arm. "Where are you going, young lady?"

Grandma Bess. "I. . .I need some air." Josie stumbled over her words.

"You've got too much grit to turn tail and run now. Straighten up and show some backbone." Grandma Bess folded her arms, her ever-present valise banging against her waist.

How easy for Grandma to say, but just being in the same room with Eli and knowing he was lost to her forever was more than Josie could bear. What if they had met under other circumstances? What if she had told him the truth from the very beginning? What if he had believed her about Fox? What if, what if, what if?

The words pounded through her, leaving her aching and empty. When Eli responded to the calls for a speech, the lump in her throat grew so large she couldn't draw breath. *Lord, I can't do this. I know You've forgiven me, but having Eli doubt me. . . I just can't do this. Help me get out of here.*

Grandma Bess blocked the door.

"Ladies and gentlemen," Eli's voice cut through her like a hot knife, "no doubt you're expecting me to make some sort of eloquent speech praising myself and Kennebrae Shipping. But I'm not going to do that. Instead, I want to tell you about the person truly responsible for our victory." Eli stepped up on the hearth and scanned the crowd.

Josie couldn't help but stare at his handsome face, so earnest and alive.

"As you've no doubt heard, the *Keystone Vulpine* went down today in rough seas due to a design flaw. Though we at Kennebrae Shipping regret the loss of the ship and her cargo, we are grateful that no lives were lost. If I had had my own way, the *Bethany*, too, would've been built with these same design flaws, and the crews of two ships might have died today. Tragedy was averted due solely to the efforts of a brave young woman. Because she refused to bow to convention, refused to let stubborn men stand in her way, she corrected the flaw in my design and was brave enough to point it out when she noticed it on the *Vulpine*. If she hadn't exhibited such courage, the *Bethany* wouldn't have been in place to rescue her adversary's crew when they were in distress. Many lives would've been lost."

Josie blinked, her mouth going dry.

The guests looked at one another, puzzlement clear on their features.

"But that isn't what I most wanted to say about this remarkable young woman."

His eyes bored into hers across the room, compelling her to listen. She twisted her fingers harder, her knees quivering.

"This woman, beyond being the most capable engineer I've ever known, is beautiful, gentle, and caring. She has integrity and honor, and her loyalty knows no bounds. She's generous and forgiving." His gaze became warm, a smile playing about his mouth. "At least, I *hope* she's forgiving. You see"—he spread his hands in a gesture of appeal—"I've been an idiot where she's concerned. I didn't realize what a treasure I had until it slipped from my grasp. I treated her badly, and yet she didn't return hurt for hurt. She did the right thing when she broke our engagement."

Mama gasped, and Father pivoted to gape at her.

Josie wanted to sink through the floor. Did he have to announce their broken engagement before all of Duluth society?

But Eli wasn't finished yet. "I only hope she can forgive me yet again and accept the gift of my love. I'll never love another, for there's only one Josie." He stepped off the hearth and started toward her.

The crowd parted before him.

"When I asked you to marry me before, it was for all the wrong reasons. Now I'm asking you for the only right one. Forget about families, forget about contracts and ships and obligations. Put aside meddling grandfathers and blueprints and secret identities and all the things that have come between us, and know this. . .I love you, Josie Zahn. Will you marry me?"

Every head in the room swiveled to stare at her, but she couldn't take her eyes off Eli. Shock and disbelief welded her feet to the ground. Finally, Grandma Bess gave her a little push to get her started. Her legs shook with every step.

Eli met her halfway.

She stopped before him, staring up into his face, afraid to let go of the guard around her heart and believe his declaration. She didn't realize she was gripping her fingers tight until he eased them apart. The warmth of his touch penetrated her chill, and she looked down. The opal ring she'd so loved, that she'd dreamed of him putting on her hand, slipped onto her finger.

He cupped her face, his eyes imploring, full of love and remorse. "This ring comes with a couple of strings attached, you know."

"Strings?" The word came out a whisper, all she could muster under the circumstances.

He nodded. "Yeah. It comes with my heart. I'm useless without you. I love you, Josie. And I need to hear that you love me, too, and that you forgive me for being such an imbecile."

She blinked back tears that thickened her voice. "You're forgiven, Eli. I love you, too."

"Marry me?"

"Yes."

He folded her into his embrace, crushing her to him and bringing his lips down to hers.

All the hurt and misunderstanding, the uncertainty and guilt, washed away in the wonder of his love. She returned his embrace, giving and accepting love and forgiveness with her whole heart.

He raised his head but didn't release her as applause broke out around them.

Josie could barely breathe for the happiness welling up inside her.

Guests pressed forward to wish them well.

Eli kept his arm around her waist and, in a lull, pressed a kiss against her temple and whispered, "We'll sort everything out later, love."

A shiver raced up her spine, and she wondered if he would always affect her this way. "As long as you love me, there's nothing more that needs sorting out."

He squeezed her waist and kissed her again. His eyes took on a twinkle, and he inclined his head toward the fireplace.

Grandma Bess had taken a chair next to Mr. Kennebrae. Their white heads bent close together. "What do you suppose he's up to now?"

She giggled, happiness breaking over her again. "Plotting baby Matthew's engagement?"

Eli laughed. "We should turn the tables on him. I think your grandmother and my grandfather would make a nice couple, don't you?"

"Another Kennebrae-Zahn wedding? I think that's a wonderful idea."

A Letter To Our Readers

Dear Reader:
In order that we might better contribute to your reading enjoyment, we would appreciate your taking a few minutes to respond to the following questions. We welcome your comments and read each form and letter we receive. When completed, please return to the following:

Fiction Editor
Heartsong Presents
PO Box 719
Uhrichsville, Ohio 44683

1. Did you enjoy reading *The Engineered Engagement* by Erica Vetsch?
   ❑ Very much! I would like to see more books by this author!
   ❑ Moderately. I would have enjoyed it more if

   _____
   _____
   _____

2. Are you a member of **Heartsong Presents**? ❑ Yes ❑ No
   If no, where did you purchase this book? _____
   _____

3. How would you rate, on a scale from 1 (poor) to 5 (superior), the cover design? _____

4. On a scale from 1 (poor) to 10 (superior), please rate the following elements.

   _____ Heroine   _____ Plot
   _____ Hero   _____ Inspirational theme
   _____ Setting   _____ Secondary characters

5. These characters were special because? _____

_____

_____

6. How has this book inspired your life? _____

_____

_____

7. What settings would you like to see covered in future
   Heartsong Presents books? _____

_____

_____

8. What are some inspirational themes you would like to see
   treated in future books? _____

_____

_____

9. Would you be interested in reading other **Heartsong
   Presents** titles? ❏ Yes ❏ No

10. Please check your age range:
   ❏ Under 18   ❏ 18-24
   ❏ 25-34   ❏ 35-45
   ❏ 46-55   ❏ Over 55

Name _____

Occupation _____

Address _____

City, State, Zip _____

E-mail _____

Presents